THE FRIEND OF WOMEN

AND OTHER STORIES

Books by Louis Auchincloss

Fiction

The Indifferent Children
The Injustice Collectors
Sybil
A Law for the Lion
The Romantic Egoists
The Great World and Timothy Colt
Venus in Sparta
Pursuit of the Prodigal
The House of Five Talents
Portrait in Brownstone
Powers of Attorney
The Rector of Justin
The Embezzler
Tales of Manhattan
A World of Profit
Second Chance
I Come As a Thief
The Partners
The Winthrop Covenant
The Dark Lady
The Country Cousin
The House of the Prophet
The Cat and the King
Watchfires
Narcissa and Other Fables
Exit Lady Masham
The Book Class
Honorable Men
Diary of a Yuppie
Skinny Island
The Golden Calves
Fellow Passengers

The Lady of Situations
False Gods
Three Lives: Tales of Yesteryear
The Collected Stories of Louis Auchincloss
The Education of Oscar Fairfax
The Atonement and Other Stories
The Anniversary and Other Stories
Her Infinite Variety
Manhattan Monologues
The Scarlet Letters
East Side Story
The Young Apollo and Other Stories
The Friend of Women and Other Stories

Nonfiction
Reflections of a Jacobite
Pioneers and Caretakers
Motiveless Malignity
Edith Wharton
Richelieu
A Writer's Capital
Reading Henry James
Life, Law and Letters
Persons of Consequence:
Queen Victoria and Her Circle
False Dawn: Women in the
Age of the Sun King
The Vanderbilt Era
Love Without Wings
The Style's the Man
La Gloire: The Roman Empire
of Corneille and Racine
The Man Behind the Book
Theodore Roosevelt
Woodrow Wilson
Writers and Personality

THE

FRIEND *of* WOMEN

AND OTHER STORIES

Louis Auchincloss

Houghton Mifflin Company

BOSTON   NEW YORK

2007

For information about permission to reproduce selections from
this book, write to Permissions, Houghton Mifflin Company,
215 Park Avenue South, New York, New York 10003.

Visit our Web site: www.houghtonmifflinbooks.com.

Library of Congress Cataloging-in-Publication Data

Auchincloss, Louis.
  The friend of women and other stories / Louis Auchincloss.
    p. cm.
  ISBN-13: 978-0-618-71866-5
  ISBN-10: 0-618-71866-4
  1. Upper class—Fiction. 2. Rich people—Fiction. I. Title.
  PS3501.U25F75 2007
  813'.54—dc22   2006011044

Book design by Anne Chalmers
Typefaces: Janson Text, Linotype-Hell Didot

Printed in the United States of America

MP 10 9 8 7 6 5 4 3 2 1

For
VIRGINIA DAJANI,
imaginative and resourceful executive director
of the American Academy of Arts and Letters

Contents

1

L'Ami des Femmes

· 1 ·

2

The Devil and Rufus Lockwood

· 67 ·

3

The Call of the Wild

· 94 ·

4

The Conversion of Fred Coates

· 104 ·

5

The Omelette and the Egg

· 135 ·

6

The Country Cousin:
A Comedy in One Act

· 174 ·

The Friend of Women

AND OTHER STORIES

L'Ami des Femmes

I.

I LIKE TO THINK of myself as *l'ami des femmes*, although in a longish life—I am now sixty—I have never married, nor even (though I hardly glory in it) had a love affair. But as a confirmed bachelor and head of the English department at Miss Dickerman's Classes, the finest, at least in my opinion, of Manhattan's private day schools for young ladies, I have made it my lifework to convince my pupils that there is nothing that men can do, outside of the mindless fields of violent sport and physical combat, that women cannot do as well or even better. In this year 1960 (I share the age of the century), the realization of such an ideal is much more widely shared than when I started preaching it, but in the nineteen thirties, the period treated in this memoir, it had still a long road to travel.

Obviously, at least to any devotee of French drama, the name I give myself is taken from the play of Dumas *fils* in which the protagonist dedicates himself to the task of saving a married woman, trapped in what she has deemed an incompatible union, from taking a lover. He believes, like La Rochefoucauld, that the wife who has taken but one lover in her life is a rare being, and that the first misstep inevitably entails successors. No doubt contemporary mores have left Dumas *fils* and myself behind, as dead as the dodo. Dumas is remembered today only because Verdi made a beautiful opera out of one of his plays, and he himself came to realize the inevitable doom of a double standard established by an aristocratic *désoeuvré* society, where the men were engrossed with seduction and hunting and their neglected wives left with nothing but children and the small satisfaction of their own chastity. And when he at last advocated that men also should be virgins until marriage, he was no longer taken seriously. Both sexes had opted for liberty in what they chose to call love.

My difference from Dumas's hero is not that I am any less the friend of women, but that I do not see their problem so much as subjection to the laws of men as subjection to men themselves. Sex is their danger, and freedom to indulge in it only makes it more so. It is not that I think it should hold no role in their lives, but that it should play a much smaller one than it does. Very much smaller.

There! I've said it. I have articulated the greatest heresy of our time. The first thing a modern biographer wants to know about his subject is what was his sex life like. And if there doesn't seem to have been one, as in my own, what is he repressing? Is he homosexual? Well, call me neuter. The beauty I have passionately sought all my life has been in literature, which I have tried to share with those young persons most open to it. It was not in football or baseball fields that I found my sharers.

Am I really so odd? It wouldn't have seemed so in the past. Religions all over the world have seen untold numbers of men and women devote themselves to chastity; sects have existed that shunned all forms of sexual union. My message to women has been, See first and foremost what you can do to make something of yourself, free of any other human being.

That accomplished, let husbands and children come as they may.

If I say so myself, I have been a popular teacher at Miss Dickerman's Classes. I have now served under three headmistresses, the last and longest tenured of whom treats me as a kind of first minister and consults with me on every change in school policy. The trustees regard me as a desirable extra man for their dinner parties, and mothers of my students seek my advice, sometimes embarrassingly, as to their daughters' personal problems. I enjoy the reputation, certainly exaggerated, of being so rapt by poetry that I sometimes have one eye on a page of Keats or Shelley as I walk to school in the morning, and I have often felt the unsought grip of a friendly pupil's hand on my elbow as I cross a street. At Christmastime I have had to let it be known that I would accept no gifts from students, to avoid the flow of ties, scarves, and sweaters that would otherwise cover my desk. And I have kept up with my girls even after their graduation; I have attended multitudes of weddings and acted as godfather to many a baby daughter.

But of course there are girls who have been special. I formed a little club of students who wanted to read books over and above what their courses required, and we met at my tiny brownstone in the East Seventies on Saturday mornings to discuss the volume chosen for the week, a practice entirely independent of the school curriculum and for which I received no emolument other than my own joy in it. And it was from these gatherings that I formed my friendships with three girls that have been the three closest relationships of my life, excepting only that with my late, lovely, long widowed mother, whose only and cherished child I had the great good fortune to be. It is to review for my own stern edification the benefit or the damage I may have done these three women that I am writing this memoir. The audience is myself alone.

Readers of Henry James's ghost story "The Turn of the Screw" have much debated whether the governess who narrates the tale actually saw the ghosts that seem fatally to threaten the children or whether they are the figments of her diseased imagination. Is she saving the children from tragedy or causing it herself? Was I the bewitched or the witch?

My three young ladies, all members of the senior class of 1937 at Miss Dickerman's, were intimate friends with one another. Indeed, they called themselves the three musketeers, as in the famous novel of my favorite playwright's father. What brought them to me was the hope they shared to find in fiction or poetry a life beyond the somewhat narrow and conventional existence for women envisioned by the Miss Dickerman's Classes of that day. They were by no means radical; the Great Depression, which had only lightly scarred their families, had not moved them to communism or even socialism. Their common passion was to express themselves, their real selves. Or what they wanted their real selves to be.

They were Alfreda Belknap, of a decent but unremarkable old New York clan; Cora King, daughter of a famous Manhattan salon hostess; and Letitia "Letty" Bernard, heiress of the Jewish millionaire Elias Bernard, prominent member of "our crowd."

To describe them individually, Alfreda Belknap presented a neat, clean, and orderly if somewhat demure appearance to a world of which she was always keenly conscious. You saw at once that she was striving to make a good impression. She was not quite as pretty as she seemed at first: her turned-up nose was a trifle too small and her chin a bit too cleft, but her total effect had a winsome charm, and her clothes (she never wore the ugly green school uniform when she came to my house) were, as even the much more casually arrayed Cora King reluctantly admitted, in the best possible taste. If I were writing a modern version of *Little Women* (which I certainly hope I'm not), I would say she was our Amy. The Belknaps were solid, mildly prosperous brownstone bourgeois—Alfreda's father a lawyer, her mother active on charitable boards—who led a sensible and mundane existence, very much deemphasizing the more glittering memory of Mrs. Belknap's parents, who had belonged to the epicurean expatriate world of Paris in the *belle epoque* until they lost their fortune in the Wall Street panic of 1907.

I mention this last because it was so important in Alfreda's spiritual development. She shared in no way her family's stern repudiation of what they deemed a life of false values that had cost them an inheritance, and seemed determined to reconstitute, insofar as she should be able, the elegant and polished manners of her grandparents' social circle where, as she saw it, artists and writers had mingled decorously with nobles of the old faubourg. She envied Cora King the latter's mother's salon, which Cora hated. Yet Alfreda was no fool. She recognized perfectly that the world about her had turned to cruder pleasures and cruder language, but she saw no reason that older values should not, at least for a privileged minority, be revived. And she had a formidable willpower to accomplish anything she chose.

What did she hope to get out of me? And out of Cora King and Letty Bernard? Of course she was intrigued by Cora's beauty and Cora's mother, even if Cora seemed to value these less. And anybody might cast a covetous eye at Letty's wealth. But I think her main object was to attain, with two other students to help, the culture that might stand her in good stead if she should ever be able to take a lead in a society that was to be intellectually as well as socially prominent. She may have dreamed of becoming a political hostess like the Princess Lieven, moving in the courts to which the Russian czar sent her husband as envoy. I know she had studied a life of that lady.

Cora King was quite her opposite. The poor girl had been made to feel a bore in her mother's brilliant salon, where wit and repartee trumped youth and beauty, and where age had little patience with the stammering or the tongueless. Her popularity with her own contemporaries should have made up for this, but it didn't. Cora was what Dante Gabriel Rossetti would have called a stunner: she had a splendid figure, firm and tall, and a wonderful flowing mane of golden hair. Yet she had been somehow undermined by lack of appreciation at home. She was careless in her demeanor, in her dress, in her talk; she lounged in chairs and was critical and easily discouraged. But she had a big heart and a generous nature, and, however suspicious she might be of any who sought to befriend her, she yearned for love and to be loved. I believe that her strong attachment to myself sprang from my making her feel that she had as much to give the world as any of her mother's snooty friends. And she almost did. There was a brain behind all that blond allure, if one could only get at it.

Letty Bernard was certainly the brightest of my trio; she had a first-class intellect and knew it. She was perfectly clear as to what she wanted from me: the school was not filling her to capacity. That was not the fault of the school, nor did she blame the school—her capacity was endless. She simply pumped everything I had out of me, and I loved it. She was a plain girl with a round, bland face and dark hair brushed straight back and a short plump body, but she moved with grace and dignity. She was quite conscious of being the only Jewish girl in her class (these were the days of secret quotas), but she seemed neither to minimize the fact nor resent it. Like Margaret Fuller, she accepted the universe. She appeared to take no false pride in her father's wealth; she respected him deeply as a philanthropist and was fully prepared to become one herself when the time should call. She had great kindness, and I think she saw in Cora a chance to help the girl make more of herself. What she saw in Alfreda I could never quite make out, but they seemed good friends. Letty might have been our Meg had she been gentile and gentler. But she was too strong for that. And we had no Beth. All three of my girls enjoyed rude health.

To give an example of how the trio devoured Victorian fiction, I shall try to reconstruct a weekend discussion at my tiny brownstone on a mews near the East River in their last school year. The topic was "Your favorite heroine of the era."

ALFREDA (*with modulated enthusiasm*): Oh, that's an easy one for me. Elizabeth Bennet, in *Pride and Prejudice*. She has the same charm for everyone, high or low. Even for Mr. Collins. And Darcy's pride goes down like ninepins before it.

ME: She is indeed enchanting. Yet a realist, too, like her father and not like her idiotic mother.

CORA (*perhaps finding Alfreda a bit prim*): Maybe Elizabeth's a bit too much of a realist. Doesn't Darcy's great house and garden play a role in her affection for him? You will remember, Alfie, that when Jane asks her how long she has loved Darcy, she replies that it dated from her first sight of his beautiful gardens at Pemberley.

ALFREDA: But she was only joking!

LETTY (*judiciously*): Still, Cora may have a point, Alfie. My father used to say that if you take everything said in jest literally, you'll be right as many times as you're wrong. When a man jokes, "I'd like to kill my mother-in-law!" he may mean just that.

ALFREDA: And even if Elizabeth *was* motivated in the least bit by Darcy's great position in the world, where's the harm? She knew that he needed a woman with taste and moderation to run his households and that she herself would be just the person. She had seen in his aunt, Lady Catherine, how badly the rich often do it.

CORA: Is that what you would think, Alfie, if you were courted by a millionaire?

ME: Girls, girls, let's not be personal.

LETTY: What Cora is suggesting could, of course, be true of anyone. There are imps in our souls of whom we are not even aware. Sometimes they emerge when we're old and senile. I had a great aunt who had lived a life of the severest virtue. No untoward word or phrase was ever heard from her lips. But when she became incompetent she suffered from an illusion that she had been captured by the Barbary pirates and sold to the proprietor of a house of ill fame. Her language was such that her doors had to be closed to all but the immediate family.

ME: Dear me, shall we get back to Miss Austen? Cora, who is your favorite?

CORA: Cathy Earnshaw in *Wuthering Heights.* She was married to the proper Edgar Linton, but her love was all for Heathcliff.

ALFREDA (*shuddering*): But he was a monster!

CORA: A monster with sex appeal, Alfie. You can see why Isabella Linton went off with him even after he strangled her little dog.

ALFREDA (*to Letty*): Cora's giving us the example of the beauty and the beast. She prefers the jungle because her beauty would give her the advantage over you and me. All the beasts would go for her, of course.

CORA: Thanks, Alfie, for the Irish compliment!

ME: Ladies, please! Letty, will you give us your candidate?

LETTY: Let me say one more thing first about Cathy Earnshaw. I share Cora's sympathy for her. Her dilemma is a hopeless one. She sees that Edgar Linton is a better man and a better husband than the savage Heathcliff could ever be, and that a marriage to Heathcliff would be a social disaster for her. Yet there she is: Heathcliff has her soul. It's a pitiable situation, and death seems the only solution.

ME: So she's not your favorite.

LETTY: No, Jane Eyre is. She's so straight and clear-visioned and firm. So modest, yet so proudly independent. And so brave. I love the way she stands up to Mr. Rochester's bullying.

ALFREDA: I agree about her, but isn't the novel too full of exaggerations? There's something so violent about the Brontës. Would the daughter of a peer really rebuke a servant with "Cease thy chatter, blockhead, and do my bidding!"

ME: But I love that! It's so Charlotte Brontë! No one else would have written it.

LETTY: And who's to say it's exaggerated? The Brontës had governesses—they knew the score.

———

In writing about my girls I obviously can choose any technique I prefer, but it is impossible for a teacher of English literature not to be very much aware of the points of view. Can I possibly forget that I am the Hubert Hazelton who wrote that little study (forgotten, alas, by everyone else) "The Styles of the Master"? And did James not condemn the first-person narrator? I may not be writing fiction, yet to some extent all writing is fiction. I can certainly use the art of the novel for part of what I shall write about Cora and Letty, for I think I have some "in" as to what they might say in my absence, but Alfreda is more of a mystery, and I can set down only my speculations.

Anyway, I shall start with Alfreda, for she is the only one of the trio whom I knew before I had her in a class. Her parents summered, as they put it, in Bar Harbor, Maine, where I too used to spend July and August in a rented room at the DeGregoire Hotel. As a bachelor who knew members of the summer colony who had daughters at my school, I received frequent invitations to dinner parties, some of which I found tedious but, as the representative of an academy at least partially dependent on their bounty, I hesitated to decline. I know it was something of a joke among the more liberal visitors to that enchanted island that my "kill off" dinner, given at the end of the season at the Pot and Kettle Club, was the best fun of the summer, as at the last minute I found I could not bear to invite all the bores who had wined and dined me and instead confined myself to the much more amusing folk who hadn't.

Mrs. Belknap, Alfreda's mother, was a very sensible woman, not at all one of the summer bores, though a bit on the dry side, and I went with considerable pleasure to her shingled villa on the Shore Path where I met her then six-teen-year-old daughter. Alfreda was small, dark eyed and dark haired, reserved, and pretty, and dressed with a fashionable neatness that seemed more of her own taste and choosing than that of her rather plain and sober parent. Her conversation was advanced for her age, precise and a bit formal. She was very much the young lady. When I called one afternoon and found her mother out, Alfreda invited me to stay for tea and presided over the table like a practiced hostess. But she was intelligent and, unlike so many of her contemporaries, already had a clear concept of the woman she wanted to be.

"I know it sounds odd," she replied in answer to my question, "but I think what I'd like would be to find myself in a position in life where I'd be among the people who make the world go round."

"And would you be giving it a push of your own?"

"In a way. But the great thing would be to be there."

"You mean, as the wife of some great man?"

"Well, that would help, of course. But what I really mean is that I'd like to be able to shed some degree of influence. And not just on one man, but on more than one, and women, too. There's much talk these days of women's rights, and that's well and good, but I'm still old-fashioned enough to think that the greatest effect that women can have on things is through their effect on men."

"You mean romantically?"

"Well, that's one way. But not the one I'm thinking of. I was thinking more of women as a necessary supplement to men. As stimulating ideas and projects that men might not realize without them."

"In what way?"

"Well, one way might be to create an attractive milieu for the exchange of ideas."

"Like a salon?"

"Something like that. I believe uptown should be just as important as downtown. And a dinner party as productive as a conference room. I want to prepare myself for some such role. That's why I'm so glad to be an eleventh grader this fall. I'll be able to take your English course. Everyone says you have a wider vision of culture than any other teacher."

"Heavens! Well, you'll be very welcome."

She proved almost at once to be one of my star pupils, and soon joined Cora and Letty at our weekend gatherings.

When the question arose, after Alfreda's debutante year, as to where she would best find the right matrimonial material, it came as something of a surprise to me, but not to the Bar Harbor summer community, that she did not go further afield. The Belknaps were hardly an adventurous clan and seemed always to have been satisfied with the company of relatives and neighbors. And Tommy Newbold was a man whom everybody liked. He had messy blond hair, laughing blue eyes, and a strong, short, stocky figure; he joked about everything, sometimes a bit tiresomely but with an infectious good humor that nothing seemed able to quell. And yet he was reputed to be a shrewd and capable lawyer with a bright future in the great Wall Street firm for which he clerked. His family occupied a summer villa next to the Belknaps, and he had been "sweet on" his prim, pretty little neighbor from an early date. She must have seen greater possibilities in him than I did, though I by no means underrated him. But would he make the world go round?

They made, it was true, a somewhat incongruous pair.

Where she was so neat and dainty, presiding over the younger gatherings at her parents' house with grace and precision, he was a rather fumbling sort, apt to spill a drink or slump too heavily in a delicate chair or even tell an off-color story to a prudish aunt. Yet he worshipped Alfreda; he seemed indeed almost in awe of her. She was always a little princess in his adoring eyes. She must have imagined that he was the kind of clay she could handle. Had she been a teacher as I was, she might have recognized that there were clays capable of resisting the deftest hands.

They started well enough after a big stylish wedding at St. James's in New York and a honeymoon in Majorca. Tommy soon became a partner in his firm, and Alfreda, in a few years' time, was known about town for her elegant dinner parties in their small but exquisite penthouse on Park Avenue. She certainly did things well. Her food and wine were fine, her decoration tasteful, and she was clever in bringing people out, in making them talk. But there was no concealing from so close and interested an observer as myself that our hostess was not as satisfied with her achievement as her guests. The reason came out one evening when she had selected me to chat with after dinner. I had just congratulated her on the congeniality of the group she had assembled.

"There are too many lawyers," she complained. "Tommy always has his list of musts. And when they're not lawyers, they're clients. In Tommy's world people dine out only to eat, drink, and talk shop. They have no interest in the exchange of ideas. Or of a social gathering as the soil in which the finest things can grow. I suppose they're all as American as apple pie. But I sometimes wonder how long I can stand it, Hubert."

"You're not really serious, Alfreda?"

"I've never been more so!"

"Then you've been dreaming, I suppose, of some kind of brilliant salon. Perhaps like Cora's mother's?"

"Well, something of that sort. It was part of my old credo that a woman's role is to make something of a man. Have I just been a fool?"

"No. But you may have been born at the wrong time. And in the wrong place. Women are thinking today that their role is to make something of women."

"Which to me is the same thing. But Tommy is perfectly content to remain exactly what he is. He doesn't want to change a thing about himself except to become a better and better lawyer."

"Which he will be," I replied in stout defense of her worthy spouse. "You may find yourself the wife of a famous judge one day, my dear."

"And what will I be? An old, dull woman, the recipient of a million legal anecdotes. What can I make of a man who's already made himself?"

I was only left to hope that if Alfreda didn't have a husband who could be fashioned into the man of her dreams, she might have a son or sons whom she could work on, but as time went by and no offspring appeared, I began to wonder if they ever would. *Les petits ducs se font un peu attendre*, as my beloved Dumas *fils* wrote of the barren marriage of the duc and duchesse de Septmonts in a late play.

2.

I have followed Alfreda's life up to marriage, and I shall do the same with Cora King and Letty Bernard before enlarging upon the bitter crises that awaited all three in the early years of wedlock. Because I have always emphasized the great things that women can do without the assistance or even the presence of men, I do not wish to be taken as downgrading my own sex or exaggerating the problems of finding a worthy husband. All of my girls might easily have made happier matches. The only thing wrong with Tommy Newbold was that he wasn't the right man for Alfreda. Luck plays a major role in matrimony.

Cora King was something of a lost soul when she graduated from Miss Dickerman's Classes. She should, of course, have gone to college, but she stubbornly refused to take the exams. I suspect this was because she feared failing all but English lit and dreaded the humiliation. It was certainly true that her grades in history and mathematics were dismal—only in my course did she excel. Like Alfreda and Letty she was an avid reader of fiction and poetry. She had even struck me at moments as being almost frantic to escape from a world in which she felt somehow inadequate to the world of her imagination.

When I urged her to at least take a course at Columbia, she demurred, telling me that she wanted all her time for the composition of a novel. And indeed she wrote one, the dreary tale of a jaded debutante who has a tumultuous affair with a gangster, modeled no doubt on her adored Heathcliff. Of course she gave it to me to read, and of course I had to tell her, as gently as I could, that it wouldn't do.

Her reaction was violent. Instead of working on the drastic revisions that I had suggested, she burned the manuscript and vowed to write never again.

"I suppose it's just as well I found out young that I was

no good," she moaned. "Otherwise I might have wasted my whole life trying."

I was very much afraid that she was headed toward the wasting of her life in any case. She saw less of Alfreda now that the latter was married and absorbed in what Cora rather scornfully referred to as her "neat little housekeeping," and Letty, though always friendly and hospitable, was now very taken up with her studies at Barnard. Cora was the financially unendowed only child of a second marriage; unlike her older and richer half-sisters, she was entirely dependent on her mother and lived at home. She did have a couple of love affairs, not as usual before World War II as now, but hardly surprising in view of her loneliness and stunning appearance. Neither, however, worked out. One was with an older married man, a painter whom she met at one of her mother's gatherings, and who broke it off roughly when a former mistress wanted him back. It simply confirmed her idea that her mother's guests found her good for only one thing. The other was a homosexual poet who was trying to persuade himself that he not what he manifestly was, and poor Cora insisted, typically, that her own ineptitude as a lover was the real cause of the tepidity of his performance. I began to think of her as a splendid but lonely lioness deprived of her pride—a word I use in two senses.

I think I was close enough to Cora, whom I loved the most of my three, to continue my version of her story as though I were writing a novel. I am bold enough to hope that my reconstruction of conversations that I did not hear bears a sufficient resemblance to what may have actually been said.

Cora always felt that her particular stumbling block in life had been that she had been brought up not in a home but in a salon. Her father, like his predecessor, had been divorced when she was three, and her mother, thereafter single, had been totally preoccupied with her gatherings. Alexia Gordon King—she always preserved the name, although only as a middle one, of the multimillionaire first husband she had long ago shed—was the renowned hostess of a famed salon that met on alternate Thursday evenings in her double brownstone mansion in Manhattan's Murray Hill. There the talked-of writers, artists, and musicians of the day mingled freely with the more liberal politicians and the more open-minded of the old Knickerbocker society. Alexia had no special artistic genius of her own, but she had an unerring eye and ear for what was at least provocative in the new and, above all, a magnificent self-confidence that enabled her to push open any closed door and to demand—successfully—the impossible of anyone whose intellectual pocket she chose to pick.

Cora's mother, who noticed everything, was quite aware not only of her daughter's deficiencies, but of her daughter's awareness of them, and she was quite smart enough to perceive that the latter was the more truly harmful. The trouble was that when she had time to correct a child, which was rare enough, she did it with the sharpness of a professional dramatics coach at a rehearsal. She probably considered this a compliment to the child.

"You think too much about yourself, Cora. You're always fretting about what's the right thing to say. I've watched you, my dear, even when you've no idea that I am. A hostess learns how to do that. Self-consciousness makes one awkward. You've got the right looks, the right appearance. Use them. Get into the person you're talking to. Forget about Cora King and the impression she's making. It doesn't so much matter what you say as how you say it. Every professional comedian knows that. Of course that doesn't mean you can say dumb things. Just learn to be silent about what you know nothing about. I heard you the other night, when you told Irving Berlin that your favorite of his songs was 'Over There.'"

Indeed Alexia had always seemed to be within earshot every time a gaffe was made. But there had been compensations in Cora's life. The attention she received from boys at any mixed party of her own age was certainly flattering. But that sort of thing, she had strongly suspected, was trivial, or at least of minor importance in her mother's greater world. She had not seen a place for herself of her very own until she had been invited to join a reading group of girls at school.

This had come about from a seemingly unlikely source. Alfreda Belknap had appeared her opposite in every respect: small, neat, and orderly. But Alfreda's inclinations were not all shaped by her discriminating taste. She had succumbed to a violent crush on Cora, sitting by her in class and whispering to her even in silent study periods. Cora accepted this with a rather benign indifference, but her enthusiasm was at last aroused when Alfreda directed her reading away from the detective stories that she had favored and focused her attention on *The Idylls of the King*. The next year Cora went on to Jane Austen and the Brontës and was introduced to the poetry of Keats and Shelley by the more serious Letty Bernard, who had accepted her as a now necessary appendage of her pal Alfreda. The "three musketeers" were soon a special trio at Mr. Hazelton's once-a-week.

What these meetings did for Cora was give her a sense of having a milieu of her own that was not only utterly independent of her mother's exclusive and excluding salon, but that, in its own small way, had elements in common with it. Mr. Hazelton himself had on more than one occasion been asked to a gathering of Alexia's, and he had spoken of it to Cora in terms that did not suggest it was Olympia but merely an agreeable medium for the exchange of views.

"Would you like to be a great hostess like your ma?" Alfreda had asked Cora one day, as they walked home from a Hazelton meeting. "A Madame Recamier? Greeting the arriving guest with a sighed *Enfin!* and the departing one with a regretful *Deja?*"

"I'd probably get them mixed up."

"Silly! You'd only have to look at your guests and be silent. God, if I had your looks, Cora, what couldn't I do with them?"

But time removed even this compensation from Cora's life. After graduation from Miss Dickerman's, the musketeers met much less often. Letty was busy at college, and Alfreda, cured of her teenage infatuation, was seriously dating Tommy Newbold.

Nature abhors a vacuum, and a year later a man appeared at Cora's mother's parties who showed a greater interest in her than did the other guests. Ralph Larkin, a bachelor nearing forty, a dark, heavyset, rather morose-looking man with bushy black eyebrows, heir to a Pittsburgh steel fortune, was invited to Alexia's salon as trustee of a family foundation famed for its patronage of the arts. But he did not go into society with any aim of meeting artists and writers; he had simply decided that the time had come for him to marry, and he was looking for an appropriate mate. No doubt he assumed that any girl he picked would think twice before refusing him. His air of absolute self-confidence gave him an authority that somewhat offset the sullenness of his usual expression. One felt that here at least was a man.

"Do you go in for all these longhairs, Miss King?" he asked Cora in a sneering tone.

"Well, I've got rather long hair myself, Mr. Larkin."

"Yes, but it becomes you. And I mean that."

"I'm glad I have one asset. I was beginning to wonder."

She happened to be going to a subscription dance that night, and on sudden impulse she invited him to accompany her. He was not at all like the usual stags at such parties—college men who came to dance, drink, and flirt. He frankly admitted that he came to social gatherings only to pick a young and beautiful bride from the flock. After he had danced once with Cora, he danced with no other partner.

"How many of these jamborees do you feel you have to go to?" he asked after he had firmly guided her to a lonely table in a corner for supper.

"I go to all my friends' dances, of course. Isn't that what debutantes do? Even old post-debutantes?"

"Until when? Until they've definitely nailed some poor guy?"

"Or some rich one. No, that's not it at all. That used to be the idea in my mother's debutante days. But not anymore. The last group parents want to pick a son-in-law from today is Miss Juliana Glutting's list of eligible males. That's like the telephone directory."

"What's the point then?"

"There isn't any point. Do things have to have a point? Do you have a point?"

"I do."

"Well, don't tell me about it. I have no patience with other people's points."

A woman as keen as Alexia Gordon King was not long in divining the real reason for Larkin's coming so often to her gatherings.

"Mr. Larkin seems to have an eye out for you, Cora. He's a person to keep in mind. You can always do something with a man who has character as well as money. I know he looks like a coal miner, but that's soon forgotten. He isn't wishy-washy as so many of the more epicene of my bachelors are. You know where you stand with a man like that. And never forget, my dear, that when I'm gone—and my heart is very precarious—the big Gordon trust on which we largely live will go entirely to your half-sisters. That is the way my first husband provided in his will, and as your own papa left everything he had to the little tart he left me for, you will be reduced to what I have in my own right, which is meager, to say the least."

Ralph, however, did not give her mother even the tolerably good marks she had accorded him.

"I suppose your mother's hangers-on all go home to write up her jamborees in their journals," he snarled. "They imagine historians will one day read their wet dreams as if they were Pepys or Saint-Simon. What phonies they all are!"

"Then why do you come here, Mr. Larkin?"

"One of these days I may tell you, Miss King."

Cora began to feel the excitement of a coming event in her future. Here was what her mother would describe as a "catch," and she might actually be the one to catch him! But did she want to? He had a rough sex appeal, but was that what Cathy Earnshaw felt?

But her life changed again when her mother's ended. Alexia died dramatically, as she had lived: she collapsed at one of her parties, joking and laughing in the group that she dominated, robed in gold lamé with a necklace of large emeralds. The passage of another year found the brownstone mansion sold and Cora and a young niece of her mother's reduced to living in a small apartment somewhat absurdly overfurnished with her mother's elaborate things. They were not uncomfortable, but their position in urban society was a sad contrast to what it had been. Everyone was very kind, including the enriched half-sisters, but the great world had essentially passed them by.

Ralph Larkin, however, reappeared in her life, but something in his eyes, as they took in her modest environment, seemed to proclaim, "Now I've got you, as I always knew I would!"

The idea that she might become his possession, as if, like Attila, of whom she had read in Gibbon at Mr. Hazelton's, he had a right to a captured Roman princess, considerably diminished the raw male sex appeal that she had been at least trying to see in him. She had visions of being led in triumph with a rope around her neck. Yet although her manner with him became brusquer, he did not deign to notice. He was too sure of her.

The niece, unlike her, settled down quite contentedly in their new ménage. She and Cora had a circle of old friends, mostly school or dancing class pals, with their new husbands or old beaux, conservative Knickerbocker New York, faintly dowdy, smugly satisfied with their memories of a grander past, conventional, dull, and decent. Cora found their world a stifling one, but she lacked the imagination or initiative to find one of her own.

Why had she been given nothing but the ability to attract a man she didn't really want? Why had her mother had the wonders of the world piled in her lap? And why should her mother's salon now appear to her like that dome of many-colored glass that had disappeared into the radiance of the sky, leaving Cora to a dull gray, sunless planet? When trapped at a cocktail party given by one of her cousin's boring friends, she would find herself daydreaming of the long parlor that had run the length of the old family brownstone, with its dark green tapestries and heavy, dark Renaissance chests, the room filled with chattering celebrities, where one might find oneself talking to Walter Lippmann or Helen Hayes or even Harpo Marx. Everybody was there, everybody who was anybody, and the fact that Cora King had been nobody didn't matter, as she was the only nobody in the room, which in itself was a kind of distinction.

She confided her misery to Hubert Hazelton one day at lunch.

Which gives me the clue to resume my narrative in the first person.

———

"Do you know something, Hubert?" Cora and I had long been on first-name terms. "Mother predicted just what would happen to me. It's amazing how clearly she understood me, even without being very strong in maternal affection. She should have been a writer, I suppose."

"You're right, and so I told her, at one of her gatherings she was kind enough to ask me to. But she told me she preferred to live the novel she would otherwise have written."

"Which is just what she did, damn her! Leaving not a page for a survivor to read. She took everything with her. Yet I have to admit there was a magnificence in her very selfishness. She didn't really need either of her husbands, and certainly not any of her children. They, poor things, needed people. Oh, she saw that. She thought I could make do with Larkin. Maybe she was right. What do you think?"

"Gracious me, Cora. What a question! Could you love the man?"

"I certainly don't love him now. Is that necessary?"

"Well, it certainly helps. I don't say that love is always strictly necessary, but the woman who doesn't feel it is undertaking a big job when she offers to make a man happy."

"Make *him* happy? But I want him to make *me* happy!"

"My dear girl, you're joking of course."

"Oh, Hubert, can't you stop being Thackeray for a minute? I'm deadly serious. I'm consulting you about what to do with my life!"

My thoughts became grave indeed at this. "Then don't misunderstand me, Cora. I'm being equally serious. If you marry this man with no other object than to use his wealth to solve your personal problems, you will be doing a wicked thing."

"Oh, Hubert, wicked. Wake up. This is the twentieth century we're in."

"I needn't choose to be in it. Wicked is a fine old term to remember. There's something virile in it, as opposed to lame excuses like *compulsive* or *obsessive* or *driven*."

"And you think I'd be wicked to marry Ralph?"

"Unless you were prepared—sincerely prepared—to do your best to make his life a happy one."

"You really mean that?"

"I do. My dear Cora, when your very soul is at stake, I don't beat around the bush."

"You think when I die, I'd go to hell?"

"I don't believe in hell. Except to the extent that it exists in this life for those who have risked it. Don't be one of them. Don't do this to any man. You'll live to regret it as much as he will."

"Oh, I think you'll find that Ralph can look out for himself."

"He's not my concern, Cora. You are."

"Perhaps I'd better relieve you of that. I can't bring myself to accept your credo, Hubert."

3.

For Letty Bernard, the trio on my Saturday mornings was an oasis, not exactly in a desert, but in a life that reached few things in the center of her heart. It was true that she was the only child of rich and indulgent parents; that she lived in a Beaux Arts mansion glittering with the objects that her father had captured from the Italian Renaissance; that she had a keen eye for arts and letters, but it was also true that she was endowed, or perhaps hampered, with a vision that took in her environment without the least illusion. Pale, square-faced, with straight dark hair and a strong stocky figure, Letty knew exactly what were her assets and what were her liabilities.

She knew, for example, that her slender allowance of feminine charm was only in part balanced by her wealth, that she was both fortunate and unfortunate to have been admitted to Miss Dickerman's Classes only through that elite young ladies' academy's strictly limited quota for Jewish students, that her mother was an amiable fool and that her father, overcome by her beauty, had married her, even knowing that it had taken his fortune to appease her Episcopalian family's anti-Semitism. And she also knew that her beloved male parent was a cool, calculating man, always ready to listen to a compromise.

Yet Elias Bernard occupied most of the available area of his daughter's carefully guarded heart, as she suspected that she did his. They were full partners, however undemonstrative, in a shared life, each fully aware that an impassive demeanor, a tight control of temper, a habit of checking every initial impulse, need not indicate any inability to love, to hate, to admire, or even to scorn. Elias was a handsome man, of a strong lean figure, calm, evaluating gray eyes, a firm, authoritative nose, a high, pale brow, and a receding hairline. From his office in the prominent Wall Street law firm of which he was a senior but largely inactive partner, he wisely and benevolently ruled his inherited empire: the family trust company, the vast Idaho ranch, the Bernard Foundation, and the very reputable political and scholarly quarterly the *New Orange Review*, named for an early Dutch designation of New York. Elias's goal in life, never articulated but deeply felt, was to inculcate whatever clear sense his fine mind possessed into a world sadly inclined to take the wrong turn. Through all the media available to him he tried, in every public issue, to take a rational stand.

Sometimes his daughter thought he went too far. For example, she criticized him for accepting a trusteeship of her school, thus seemingly endorsing its stingy quota for Jewish students, or even, as she put it, endorsing any quota at all.

"You know they're just after your money," she pointed out in the blunt way that attended their discussions. "They want to add a top floor for a new gym, and their drive has bogged down."

"I'm aware of that, Letty, and I'm ready to help out. They need that new gym badly. And don't forget it's a first-class school. Otherwise I'd hardly send you there, even if your mother is an alum. Eventually that quota will fall. As you know, I'm a great one for not rushing things. Time often does the trick, and a great deal of bitterness is saved."

"Like your old theory that slavery would have died a natural death without the Civil War. But would it have?"

"Wasn't saving six hundred thousand lives worth taking a chance?"

But Letty agreed with her father's sister, Aunt Rhoda, who criticized him for sometimes giving parties where no Jews were invited. At all her famous dinner parties, the very social Rhoda always included a respectable percentage of Jews — though neither she nor her brother ever entered a temple except for a wedding or a funeral. But Elias scoffed at his sister's little rule as "racist."

Letty also felt that he was wrong in preserving his marriage to her mother, though she never voiced this. She felt strongly that each of her parents would have lived a franker and freer life apart from each other. Their extreme incompatibility was painfully evident, though her father's behavior with his wife was irreproachably polite and overly considerate. Fanny Bernard had everything she wanted, and she had certainly seen to it that her life was as comfortable as money could make it, but she nonetheless chafed under the scorn that she rightly suspected her husband felt for her vanity and triviality. She was fond of Letty and liked to complain to her about all the little things that went wrong in her life, but she always knew that her daughter's firm alliance with her father constituted a bond that she could never in the slightest degree weaken, and that Letty's sympathy was based on duty and indeed on something dangerously close to pity. For Letty knew that despite her mother's fancy clothes, fine jewels, and sparkling foreign town cars, the latter would only have been truly happy had she lived in the mauve decade with other ladies in big plumed hats and Irish lace strutting down the peacock gallery of the Waldorf-Astoria.

Of course, Letty likewise knew that her own plainness in face, dress, and general attitude was distressing to her mother, but the latter had long given up trying to change her, and had learned, however regretfully, that she was not fated to play any but a walk-on role in her daughter's life and education.

Elias Bernard's concept of his civic duties made his daily and nightly routine something of a public one, with a considerable amount of entertaining done at home, all managed by a skillful housekeeper, as Fanny confined her job as hostess to striking if belated appearances, which meant that his serious talks with Letty usually had to be assigned to Sundays, when they walked in Central Park with his two greyhounds. These strolls she indeed treasured, but she needed something more, and she found it to some extent in the weekly Hazelton meetings with Alfreda and Cora. With one such day in each week, her imagination was kept from running dry.

Neither Alfreda nor Cora elected to go to college after graduating from Miss Dickerman's Classes; both made early marriages. Letty went to Barnard, where she majored in history and won a Phi Beta Kappa key her junior year. Her life seemed dedicated to serious study, and she professed to having little time for beaux and dates.

The question of her marriage was never discussed at home, but Letty had little doubt that it was very much on her father's mind. Her mother avoided the subject probably because she feared that Letty would never attract the right man or that she would turn him down if she did. The topic was therefore taboo, like any reference to the Catholic Church in the presence of Irish servants. Fanny presumably had to content herself with the prospect of her daughter becoming one of those rich, indomitable old maids who loomed so grandly and formidably over the metropolitan social scene. Letty went out occasionally with some sober young man or other from one of the respected families of "our crowd," usually one more interested in taking a brainy girl to a problem play or a concert than in getting married, and there had so far been no question of the heart.

And then at last, on one of their Sunday walks, her father spoke out.

"I am, of course, delighted, my dear, that you are doing so well at Barnard. It would be unthinkable for a woman of your intellect not to be a college graduate. But I don't want you to regard it as simply an interlude before marriage, the way your mother does. She expects a girl to quit college the moment Mr. Right appears. I want you to graduate, willy nilly."

"And I will," Letty replied stoutly. "You needn't worry about that. If Mr. Right objects, he'll soon find he's Mr. Wrong. Anyway, Mother doesn't see him as coming at all."

"There are a lot of things your good mother doesn't see. But we'll leave her out of this. How do you see a Barnard degree as affecting your life?"

"Mr. Hazelton thinks I might do well to study law. Does that strike you as wild, Papa?"

"In no way. It may be an excellent idea. The professions are opening up to women. You could perfectly well become a lawyer or doctor. But I doubt that the top positions in those disciplines are going to be available to women in your generation. These things take time. It seems to me that in your lifetime the first rank will be more apt to be open to you in partnership with a man. A big man, of course. Maybe even a great man."

"You mean like Madame de Pompadour and Louis XV? That hardly seems my role, Papa."

"No, no, no. Don't be silly. I mean as the wife of a prominent man. Consort and partner. Look at Mrs. John D. Rockefeller, Jr. Everyone knows she's the real power behind the throne."

"But, Papa, what can you be thinking of? What have I got to attract a great man? Let alone be a power behind his throne?"

"You have spirit and character, my dear. You have wit and determination. You have courage and spirit. And you're going to have money."

"Oh, money."

"Yes, money. It's time we discussed its role in your life. For you're going to be very rich, my dear, and that's something that has to be faced. I'm going to look after your mother, of course, but the bulk of my fortune is coming to you outright."

"And you're suggesting that this great man will marry me for it?"

"He will not marry you for it alone. Not if he's the right kind of great man. And I'm assuming that you'll always have the perspicacity to see through the common or garden-variety fortune hunter, no matter how blue his eyes or rippling his muscles. What you have to understand, my dear, is that worthwhile men are not likely to be motivated simply by one thing. A woman to them is a whole package of things. There are looks, to be sure, but beauty is only one factor. There's her brain, her integrity, her health, her child-bearing capacity, her congeniality, her family, her background, her tastes, and, yes, her money."

"But *you* weren't motivated by money."

"No, because I had it. I was motivated solely by the very thing I'm telling you to beware of: sexual attraction. I'll be utterly frank with you, my child. You've seen what happened between your mother and me."

Letty mused a moment over this. "Yes," she agreed with a sigh. "I have."

"We mustn't probe too deeply into a mixture of motives. What really matters is the caliber of the mate chosen. My partner, Tim Cowles, would be horrified at the very idea, but I believe that he married Anita partly because she was a great-granddaughter of Chief Justice Marshall, who was his god. And it's been a very happy marriage. All I'm saying is that your money is only one of your trump cards. But it's a trump that should be used to take a trick."

Of course now, when her father brought a handsome, twenty-nine-year-old law associate to the house to educate her in the nature and makeup of her diversified portfolio of securities, she saw in him a potential paternal candidate for her hand. Eliot Amory, scion of a distinguished Boston family, once but no longer wealthy, tall, lithe, and charmingly at ease, with smooth blond hair and eyes as blue as her father had attributed to less desirable suitors, seemed almost to be concealing a wit that was on the sharp side and a self-confidence that smacked of a sense of superiority. He was obviously what Letty, well acquainted with the young lawyers frequently brought to the house, had learned to spot as an about-to-be-made-partner, chafing at the bit.

"Is he going to be one of your great men?" she asked her father on their next Sunday walk.

"A good question. He's going places, that fellow. He has all the credentials but one. He sees himself doing whatever he's doing. Very clearly. And he's not always sure it's the right thing."

"And that's bad? Why?"

"If he grins at what he sees, it's bad. And I think Amory does. A great man should take himself seriously. A sense of humor is not what he most needs."

"Abraham Lincoln had one."

"And it hindered him. If you laugh at yourself, you're apt to underrate yourself. Lincoln would have dumped McClellan earlier if he hadn't doubted his own doubts about him. George Washington would have sacked him after Antietam."

"But, Papa, *you* have a sense of humor."

"Which may be just why I get able men to run my businesses rather than doing it myself."

Letty had occasion to see Eliot Amory in action when he tackled the job of explaining to her the myriad details of a corporate reorganization he was handling of a small company in which she and her mother were substantial shareholders. Fanny Bernard understood nothing but she listened, entranced, as he made it sound like a tale from *Arabian Nights*.

"You're like Disraeli with Queen Victoria," Letty told him when they were alone after one of these sessions. "Didn't she say he made the dullest debate in the House of Commons sound like one of his novels?"

"Weren't they both fiction, anyway? But I do it all for your ma, not for you. You grasp every detail, no matter how boring. You don't even seem to find them boring."

"Do you?"

"Well, it's my job, you know. I don't much think about whether they're boring."

"What do you hope to get from your job?"

"What does anybody?" He shrugged. "To become rich and famous. Isn't that about it?"

"You think riches bring happiness?"

"Compared to what poverty brings, yes. Haven't your riches made you happy, Letitia?"

It was the first time he had used her first name, and she liked it. It seemed suddenly to raise her to his intelligence level.

"They have not," she replied firmly. "Maybe you have to have earned them for that to happen."

"Anyway, you've learned something else. Something much more important. You've learned independence of mind."

Letty felt vaguely exuberant. "Papa wouldn't be so sure about that. He thinks I should be more realistic about money."

"That may be why he singled me out to talk to you about it."

You mean he singled you out for me, was Letty's unspoken thought. She felt the chill of something like fear.

Not long after this chat, Amory was made the youngest partner in the firm, of which some observers already speculated that he would one day be the leader.

Amory became an accepted and constant visitor at the Bernards, both in the city and in the big Tudor villa in Rye. He was not considered so much a beau of Letty's as a kind of adopted member of the family. Fanny, whom he flattered in a half serious, half joking way, adored him, while Elias continued to find him what he rarely found his business and legal acquaintances: a worthy intellectual companion. To Letty her relationship with this stimulating and sexually attractive young man was confusing. He made her feel that she was the object of his visits without ever a hint of a romantic purpose. Was she just a pal? And did she really want to be anything more?

Of course, she debated with herself as to whether or not she was falling in love. Certainly what she felt for Amory was something a good deal milder than what Cathy Earnshaw had felt for Heathcliff. However, one day when work had held him over at the firm and he failed to appear at a Sunday lunch, she had been sorely disappointed. Sorely.

Her father seemed to have gleaned something of her state of mind, for he brought up the subject quite openly on one of their walks.

"I think I should tell you, my dear, that I have settled any doubts that I may have once had about Amory. I believe now that he *is* capable of becoming a great man."

"You mean a great man for *me?*"

"Well, yes. That is, if you should want him."

"What if he doesn't want me?"

"But I think he does."

"He certainly hasn't shown it, Papa. Not that I've expected him to."

"I'm aware of that. He doesn't know how you feel about him. And, of course, he's uncomfortable about his position vis-à-vis your money. He doesn't want to look like a fortune hunter."

"Oh, Papa, there you go again. It's always the money. Have I no identity without it?"

"Listen to me, my dear." Elias paused now, and then motioned her to a bench on which they both sat, as did the dogs at their feet, always immediately obedient to their master. "We must have this out, you and I. I'm not going to be with you always. I have some reason to say so, but we won't go into that now. No, don't protest. I haven't come here to discuss my health. There's nothing to get upset about yet, so we'll drop it. But one of these days you're going to find yourself in charge of a lot of things—the magazine, the foundation, the ranch, the businesses, and even your mother. And you're going to need a competent and trusted partner. All I'm saying is that Amory could be that. He's honest, he's straight, and he's a kind of jack-of-all-trades. He approaches every problem that confronts him with an absolutely open and fresh mind. You two together could be a power in the land."

"Oh, Papa, please!" She jumped up, feeling the sudden tears in her eyes, and walked on quickly, followed by her now silent parent. Neither said a word all the way home.

The next week, sitting alone with Letty in the plant-filled conservatory after a large Sunday lunch party, Amory proposed. Coolly, quietly, earnestly. She could only gasp at first. Then she protested.

"But, Eliot, you haven't even told me that you love me!"

"I love you, Letitia, as far as my nature allows me to love. I have never loved anyone better, or as much. And I never shall."

Even at such a moment, she noted his use of the verb *shall*. It denoted simple futurity, without determination. But what if determination were not necessary for him? Why was she so prone to distrust people?

"Oh, Eliot, I don't know what to say. You'll have to give me time. Maybe a lot of time."

And she left him to rejoin the now departing guests.

The next day she dined with her old guide, Hazelton, and told me all.

"But the love he offers you isn't enough, my dear girl," I exclaimed with feeling. "It isn't nearly enough. I don't care what your father says. It isn't enough to base a marriage on!"

"But if it's all he's capable of, how can I ask for more?"

"If it's all he's capable of, he shouldn't marry at all. Or at least he should wait until he finds a girl as cool as himself. I know what I'm talking about, Letty. Believe me. There's a bit of Amory in myself. Except I have always recognized what it should limit a man to. He shouldn't offer to share his life with some deluded woman."

"And you don't think that Eliot and I between us might accomplish what Papa visualizes? Or something not too unlike it?"

"Make him your partner then. Not your husband."

Letty was a bit surprised to find how little persuaded she was by her mentor's deeply felt objections to a match between herself and Amory. After all, old dear that I was, had I any real part in the life of the great world? Had I not been content to pass my days in a quiet and protected corner? That might be well enough for me, but for her?

———

I break off my story here. Once I start speculating about what Letty thought of me and my advice, I become uneasy. The work becomes too personal, and I find myself embarrassed.

And I find it a sort of impertinence to bust my way into Letty's heart and fantasize as to what she did or didn't feel about the man she married. I should at least keep a certain distance.

I feel safe, anyway, in asserting that if Letty was strongly attracted to Amory's intelligence and personality, if she even felt a need for him as a lover, she was disturbed by his lack of anything resembling sexual passion. Oh, yes, she knew that he liked her well enough, but didn't he like even more the multitude of opportunities that marriage to her would bring? I had once pointed out that there is no intenser ambition than that felt by the young genius who's the heir of a grand old family that has fallen on evil days. The Amorys had lost their fortune in the panic of 1907. His parents had once owned the most splendid sailing yacht on the North Shore. Eliot always kept a large photograph of it on his desk.

I did, though, install sufficient doubt in Letty to induce her to postpone any decision about Amory for a year, and the following December saw our entry in World War II and Amory's departure to the Pacific as a lieutenant, JG, on a destroyer. When he returned to his firm in 1945, with a Purple Heart and a Silver Star, to find a Letty desolate with the recent loss of her father from heart failure and overwhelmed with the obligations of his estate, he had little difficulty in persuading her to join her troubled life to his. I am afraid she was even grateful to the hero for coming back to the girl who had almost rejected him.

4.

I have the three girls all married now, for Cora, of course, went ahead with her plan to become the wife of wealthy Larkin, and I have to admit that my basic distrust of all three unions put a crimp in my relationships with them. Oh, we continued our lunches, if less frequently, but our conversation was more literary than personal. The first marked return to our old ways came with Alfreda's need to consult me about her childlessness.

"We've both had all the tests," she told me. "And now we know just what it is. It's not my fault."

"Fault?" I queried. "Must there be one?"

"Biological fault, I mean." But her very definite tone did not convince me that she exempted poor Tommy of all moral responsibility. "Tommy, it appears, has a low sperm count. We have to face facts squarely, don't we, Hubert?"

"Of course. But a low sperm count doesn't mean his case is hopeless. As I understand it, it means that a pregnancy is unlikely. But not impossible."

"Hubert, I've waited four years. Isn't that what the lawyers call a reasonable time?"

"For what?"

"For me to wait. Now I must try something else."

"Like adoption?"

Alfreda made a little face. "I hate the idea of taking some other woman's unwanted baby. You may call me a snob, if you like, but I do have good blood."

Alfreda did not boast of it, but I knew how much she relished her descent from Pieter Stuyvesant. "Then there's always artificial insemination," I observed, responding to her appeal for honesty. "Would Tommy agree to that?" She nodded. "Well, at least the child would have blue blood on the distaff side."

"But what about the father?" she demanded with something like indignation, as though the whole idea had been mine.

"I believe it's usually a medical student."

"Ugh! And what do we know about *his* family? No, I can't bear the thought! That's what I've really come to talk to you about. You and nobody else, my dear old friend. Why wouldn't it make sense for me to choose the father myself? Why shouldn't we have the perfect father for the perfect child?"

"How many perfect fathers have perfect children?"

"Oh, I know all that. But at least there's a chance they will. What about the two Dumas you're always raving about? What about the two Pitts? And think of all the Adamses!"

"And when you've found this paragon, will you persuade him to donate his seed to the necessary test tube?"

"Never!" she cried. "How could I possibly ask such a man to go through so humiliating a procedure in some ghastly laboratory—probably before some leering intern?"

"It could be quite private."

"No, no! My boy would have to spring from a glorious mating!"

"Your boy? Why mightn't it be a girl?"

"Because I know it wouldn't!" She spoke with a curious passion.

"And what about Tommy? Would he agree to be a *mari complaisant?*"

"Oh, never! But he wouldn't have to know. I'd simply tell him that I'd gone through the clinical process. He'd accept the proposition that neither of us knew anything about the child's father."

"I see." But I was deeply shocked. "And this divine stud? Have you already someone in mind?"

"No," she said firmly, though her denial was preceded by a distinct pause.

"Then give up the idea. If you deceive Tommy in a matter so grave, there's bound to be a dire consequence. For him, for you, for the man you select, maybe for the child. I can't tell. All I know is that you won't get away with it. That something always happens to people who believe that the effective concealment of a crime will wash away their guilt."

Alfreda subjected me to a long evaluating stare. "So in your opinion it would be a crime?"

"It would."

She nodded, and then suddenly smiled. "Then it will be I who goes to the lab and not what you call the stud."

"Bless you, my child."

We discussed the subject no further, which is often the best way to handle a delicate problem. Alfreda never referred to it again, but her husband did. Unlike the husbands of Cora and Letty, he had always totally accepted and even encouraged my intimate friendship with his wife and actually chose to share it. "You give her things I can't, Bertie," he would tell me cheerfully. "All those books and poems you and she talk over. It's great." And he invited me to lunch at his downtown club to discuss, in Alfreda's absence, an idea he had about the product of her artificial insemination.

"The big question is whether to let it be known that Alfreda has undergone this process. Our family and friends all know that I *could* sire a child. It's just that it's unlikely. So we could take the position that the near miracle has happened, and who would there be to deny it?"

"The imps of comedy," I answered gravely. "They're always on the lookout for someone trying to get away with something. People are bound to pry when they're suspicious, and with enough prying they're apt to come up with something. Once you've made an open statement about a matter like this, they'll lose all interest in it. Believe me."

And Tommy did. But when, at a later date, I asked him how Alfreda had fared under the process, for I knew that in some cases it was accompanied by acute discomfort, he assured me that she had had none. But he also told me something disturbing. Alfreda had refused to tell him anything about what she had had to go through, or allow him to be with her on visits to the hospital, saying that the whole thing was a woman's private matter and that a husband had no role but one of possible humiliation. Recalling what Alfreda had suggested to me as a very different solution to her problem, I could hardly resist the ugly suspicion that she might have implemented it.

At any rate, she gave birth to a fine healthy boy. Everyone knew the supposed circumstances of his birth, and nobody cared, except his wise old grandmother, Mrs. Belknap, who observed to me, in her dry way, "They don't care so long as the child turns out well. But if he doesn't, they moan, 'Why the dickens did I have to get into this?' It's easier when you can lay the blame on your own inheritance. After all, there is nothing you can do about that!"

I did my best to smother my unpleasant suspicions, but two years later they received an unexpected gloss from Letty Bernard, who, to my distress, had been having some rather sharp differences with her husband over their joint management of some of the interests bequeathed to her by her father.

"Eliot seems never to tire of surprising one," she told me on one of our Central Park walks that, lacking her father, she now sometimes took with me. "Who do you think his new best friend is? Tommy Newbold!"

"Well, what's wrong with Tommy?"

"Nothing! He has a heart of gold, and we all love him. But you know as well as I, Hubert, that outside of the law, the dear man has very little to offer. Face it, he's a bore about his cases. And Eliot flees bores as he would the plague. He may be a genius, but he's a brutally intolerant one."

"But, as you say, he likes to surprise people. Eliot can't bear being taken for granted. He'll always contradict you. Tell him someone's a bore, and he'll call him a wit. A wit whom only someone as perceptive as Eliot can see. Tell him someone's a genius, and he'll call him an ass!"

"To prove you an ass. Yes, I see that. But this thing with Tommy seems a bit of a muchness."

"Hasn't Eliot been using Tommy to help him on some legal problem?"

"True. But since when did Eliot choose his friends from among his hirelings?"

Well, that was it. I wouldn't admit it to Letty for the world, but I was troubled. I had never made it a secret to myself that I disliked Eliot Amory. He simply possessed too many assets. His blond good looks, his straight, slim, sturdy build, the amiable charm of his glowing good manners, the small, intimate smile that seemed to initiate you into the inner circle of those who really knew what it was all about, the seeming effortlessness of his brilliant solution to every offered problem, all enhanced the portrait of a man with spectacular gifts. Why did I smell an arch ego behind his masterful manipulation of his wife's enterprises? Wasn't it rather mean of me to feel that only condescension lay behind his genial acceptance of his wife's old English teacher? But there you are. I did.

I now began to track the developing intimacy between Eliot and Tommy. It was true, of course, that Eliot had retained Tommy as counsel to the *New Orange Review*, which certainly necessitated a number of meetings, but why did they have to take place at the Newbolds' apartment?

The Newbolds' baby, Stephen, of whom Eliot seemed inordinately fond, was naturally his godson and the brightest and most beautiful child anyone had ever seen, but Eliot had never been a noticeably paternal type with his own two children, both daughters, and had seemed quite content with the somewhat perfunctory colloquy that he accorded the girls when the nurse brought them in for a short visit on his evening return from the office. Indeed, Letty had once confessed to me that she feared her failure to produce a son had deeply disappointed him and that she bitterly deplored the ovarian disorder that had caused her doctor to prohibit any try for a third child. Of course, she had quickly added that Eliot had never expressed a word of his regret. Like his recurrent fits of depression, he kept it to himself. The Eliot the world saw was always a cheerful one.

The crisis, as it was for me, anyway, came after a dinner at Alfreda's—just the two of us, Tommy being in Albany arguing a case—when she brought me a cognac and closed the door to the library to which we had withdrawn.

"You and I know each other so well, Hubert, that I can skip the prologue," she began. "I know what you have guessed, and I've known it for some time."

"What have I guessed?" I asked with a sinking heart.

"That my Stephen is Eliot's son."

I gasped as if I had been thrown into churning waters.

"If that is so," I finally was able to retort, "what business is it of mine? Isn't it a matter between you and Tommy and

Eliot alone? If Tommy consented to such an arrangement, mustn't it be kept the darkest of secrets? For I can't imagine that Letty knew! Mind you, I'm not criticizing you or Tommy. It may even have been, on his part, an example of his magnanimous love for you. But it must never be spoken of!"

"But Tommy would never have consented to such a thing." Alfreda's small smile seemed directed at my naiveté. "He may be brought to accept it after the fact—he might even be glad to have a distinguished father for the boy he has come to love—but he would never have consented in advance."

"Would it have made that much difference to him whose sperm was used in that tube? So long as he had to know it wasn't his?"

Alfreda rose, in a movement that suggested outrage, and strode across the room and back. "There was no question of a tube! Can you imagine Siegfried bringing a tube to Brunhild on her flaming mount? I wanted my baby to be born of a beautiful act. And he was!"

"And Tommy never knew? All right, let's keep it that way."

"But I want Tommy to know! That's what I wanted to talk to you about. I want Stephen to grow up knowing that his father and mother produced him in an act of love! I want the whole wretched subterfuge to be blown away. I want truth! And we're living in a world where these things are increasingly accepted. Eliot wants to recognize and be recognized by his son. And I'm betting that Tommy, in the last analysis, will be big enough to accept the situation which was created by his fault. No, don't look at me that way, Hubert. I know it was only a biological fault. But there you are. He will continue to be daddy to Stephen. Eliot will be simply father."

"And Letty? What will she be?"

"Letty will have all the important things. She will continue to have an important husband to share with her the important enterprises they have undertaken together. Besides, everyone knows that all has not been idyllic in the Amory household. You don't think this was Eliot's first affair, do you? He married her for her money—face it. And she knows it. She's too shrewd to upset her whole applecart by a fit of manufactured jealousy."

"It would not be manufactured. And you would not be only an unfaithful wife, Alfreda. You would have been an unfaithful friend. Never could I have believed that our old trio would end like this."

Alfreda's sudden change of expression made her whole face a gape. "Why should it end, Hubert?"

"Because I could never see you again if you go through with this."

"Oh, my god! I had no idea you'd take it this way!"

"Didn't you?"

She covered her face with her hands. She was weeping. "Oh, of course I did. You've always been our conscience, Hubert. I knew you'd never go along. And that I was wicked, wicked, wicked. All right, what do we do now?"

"Nothing. There's nothing to do. Little Stephen will do much better as people think he is than as Eliot's known bastard."

"And Eliot? Who adores the boy?"

"Can't a man adore his godson? Particularly when he has no son of his own? Never mind about Eliot. I'll keep an eye on him. Eliot is not a man, as you put it, to upset applecarts."

"And what do I do, Hubert, if in the days to come, I find myself hating you?"

"When you really love someone, my dear, as I love you three girls, you do not hesitate to incur their hate if it's for their own good."

With which I kissed her and took my discreet departure. My good deed had certainly been done for that day.

5.

Cora's marriage to Larkin started smoothly enough, or so it seemed to the casual onlooker. I assumed that Ralph, a heavy and lustful man, found adequately agreeable the couplings of their early period together. I am certainly no expert in such matters, but among my male contemporaries, I have one or two who knew Ralph moderately well and who have freely opined to me, in view of what later happened, that he might have been the kind of rough and rapid lover who derived satisfaction from coition even when his partner was only passively cooperative. But what boded really ill for the future was his too articulate chagrin at the two miscarriages that Cora suffered in the first three years of their union. Instead of the sympathy that such a disappointed mother needs, it was made very clear to her that she was expected to continue the unvarying schedule of dinner parties and sporting weekends that Ralph's Racket Club friends and their fashionable wives arranged as their refuge from any lives differing from their own. He also had a demanding and domineering old mother who expected a daughter-in-law to be constantly at her beck and call. Ralph must have been looking for an Oriental bride of complete submissiveness and thought he had found her in that lonely corner of her mother's salon. He should have foreseen that even the most passive have their moments.

I was present at an early tiff between the Larkins. I had been asked to dinner—just the three of us, in the third year of their union, during the brief period when Ralph had approved of me as a possible restraining influence on his spouse. This period did not last after he discovered that not only could I not play that role, but neither could anyone else. Cora, at the table, had asked me to support her in her expressed wish to spend the approaching summer in a villa that she proposed to rent in the south of France rather than in Southampton. Ralph had countered with his reasons for opposing her project. His tone was measured and gravelly, but not condemnatory. He evidently expected to prevail.

"Why should I wish to abandon my comfortable cottage with its well-trained staff, my sailboat, and my golf, to traipse about Europe and see palaces and cathedrals I've seen a dozen times before? Cora had a honeymoon there of two whole months. That should last any sensible woman for a few years at least."

"But we spent all last summer on Long Island," Cora protested. "And saw all the same people week after week. You've seen what it's like there, Hubert. We give a dinner of twenty one night, and the following night we meet the same twenty people at our next-door neighbors'. And they always talk about the same things! They never get tired of it, never can have too much of it. But, oh, I can!"

"I am sorry my friends don't meet your lofty intellectual standards," Ralph retorted coldly. "And that you will have to postpone your plans to scale Mount Olympus, at least for this summer. The house is being readied for us now, and I plan that we be there by June fifteenth."

"Oh, Hubert, do speak to him," Cora cried. "Tell him what *you* think of all those ghastly cocktail parties you had to go to when Alfreda had you down for that weekend."

"Why couldn't you do both?" I asked cautiously, turning to my host. "Why not take a jaunt to France in late June and then spend the balance of the summer on Long Island?"

"Because my plans have already been made, thank you" was his short rejoinder. My suggestion had not been relished.

"Well, I'll go anyway!" Cora declared. "You can have the house to yourself and entertain your head off!"

"I'll be interested to know how you plan to pay for your trip and rental in Provence."

With this he rose and left the dining room. Cora, in a rush of harsh words now explained what his last remark entailed. Ralph maintained a stiff control over their exchequer. He paid all her bills that he approved and gave her a moderate allowance for daily cash expenses, but whenever he disapproved of an item, she had to pay for it out of her own exiguous income, and that was already used up for the year. Summer travel, for that summer anyway, was out of the question.

"You could borrow, I suppose," I suggested weakly.

"He's quite capable of publishing a statement that he will not be responsible for my debts."

"Oh, Cora, surely you exaggerate!"

"You don't know him, Hubert!"

That spat, alas, was the opening gunfire of a war that would last for some three years. I hardly saw Cora more than a half dozen times in all that period, and then only at Letty's or Alfreda's, as Ralph now distrusted my influence and as Cora herself remembered too bitterly my premarital warnings and was probably afraid that I would stoop to saying "I told you so." Though I never would have.

As I put together the sorry tale of that time in her life, it appeared that the marriage was a constant struggle and Cora the constant loser. Ralph, so far as I could make out, was absolutely unyielding; he rarely even bothered to lose his temper. He simply laid down the law of where they should live and whom they should see, and refused her any funds which might have been used to introduce the least variety to their schedule. No child came to unite their interests; I suspected that separate bedrooms had been their rule. I could conclude only that Ralph was the kind of despot who was capable of deriving a grisly satisfaction in contemplating the plight of his victim. He did not, like Nero, play a lyre at the burning of Rome; he simply watched it.

It was Letty Bernard Amory who, in her practical, realistic way, proposed a solution to Cora's problem.

"I want you to help me persuade Cora to take a job, Hubert," she told me. "I've offered her a position on the *New Orange Review*, and Eliot has agreed to use her as a file clerk with the chance of rising to be a copy editor. Of course, she has no training, but she can learn. She's plenty bright enough. And we've got to get her out of that apartment where she broods all day and fights with Ralph all night."

"Won't she take the job?"

"She thinks Ralph will have a fit."

"I'll talk to him. If he'll see me."

Ralph did see me, and he gave a sullen consent to the

change in his wife's life more easily than I had expected. I supposed that even he had come to realize how badly he had misjudged his bride.

I didn't much like Cora's working for Eliot, whom I deeply distrusted, but knowing how much he resented his wife's ownership of the periodical and how little he must have liked her imposing an employee on him, I could hope only that he would give Cora a fairly wide berth. At any rate, things seemed to work themselves out, and in the next year the reverberations from the Larkin household appeared to have ceased. Cora was happy in her new job and told me that Eliot had even asked her to help him with the periodical.

The Bernards's magazine had originally been devoted to articles on politics and foreign affairs, contributed by supposed experts, but Letty and Eliot had greatly expanded its coverage. It now contained reviews of books, Broadway openings, musical events, and art shows, in addition to pieces on current events both national and international. Eliot had started a woman's page, with topics ranging from civil rights to fashion, and it was to this that he had had the keenness to promote Cora after a brief time in the files.

It seemed to Cora like a godsend. All her rather scattered wits appeared to focus in this new assignment. She had needed a cause to pull her disordered life together, and she now found it in women's rights. Perhaps Ralph had come to symbolize for her everything in the male sex that kept women down, while Eliot had become the shining light of Ralph's diametric opposite. A shabby peace had been replaced by a heroic war. She read everything about discrimination and the failure of equal treatment for women in every walk of life and came to work with shining eyes.

"I'm becoming another Carrie Nation," she exclaimed to me with a cheerful laugh. But all this came to a shuddering halt. One early morning, while I was still at breakfast, a pale and haggard Cora appeared on my doorstep. Ralph, she announced in shrill tones, wanted to divorce her, and on grounds of adultery, too! Would I accompany her to a session with his lawyer in the latter's Wall Street office? The lawyer wished to present her with Ralph's terms for a consent divorce. When I protested that she needed her own lawyer and not an old schoolteacher, she insisted that she could get hold of counsel later, that this was simply to hear Ralph's demands. She wanted a friend to be with her, someone, so to speak, to hold her hand.

So I went.

The lawyer, Stanley, I think his name was, received us in a large, threatening paneled office with a million-dollar view of the harbor for any who had the heart to look at it. I had not. He was the sort of grave, staring attorney who took pleasure on behalf of a rich client to "crush the serpent with his heel," a legal John Knox who carried his stern morals into his practice whenever his high fees allowed it.

"I take it that Mr. Hazelton is here as your friend but not as your counsel," he opened, eyeing me with evident disapproval. "However, there is no reason why I should not outline for you both your husband's proposal. It will also be contained in this memorandum, which you may deliver to your attorney."

The horrid man then proceeded to air his horrid client's conditions for submitting to the jurisdiction of the state of Nevada, where he chose to establish her temporary residence. This was clearly intended, without stating it, to indicate his client's willingness to consent to a plea of incompatibility in a Reno court. Mr. Stanley now went on to give us an idea of the evidence that his client's detectives had gathered. There was no mention of a corespondent's name, nor did Cora ask for one. Her only alternative, the lawyer implied, to a thunderous scandal would be to sign a separation agreement waiving her rights to any settlement and apply to a Reno court for a divorce on grounds of incompatibility.

She and I left the office without commitment. Despite the early hour, I took her to a bar and ordered two whiskies.

"Of course you'll fight it," I muttered.

Slowly, she shook her head.

"Tell me he's bluffing, Cora!" I begged.

"I can't tell you that."

I dreaded to hear her mention Eliot's name. I knew that he and Letty had been having difficulties about the running of the magazine. He had made little secret of his growing restiveness at her stubborn retention of the veto power that she had in the publications and foundation that her father had created. I had never trusted Eliot since the business over Alfreda's baby; indeed, I actually detested him. He had not hesitated to make himself the lover of one of his wife's most intimate friends. Could he possibly have had it in mind to add the second to his collection? Could a man really be so wicked? And why?

"You told me, Hubert, that if I married Ralph for the reason I did, I'd be wicked. I sneered at the word. But you were right. I was wicked, I am wicked. And, as you predicted, I've been in hell."

"But you've been working, Cora. You've been doing a job, and doing it darn well. What happened?"

"Everything was all right until Eliot started paying attention to me. He didn't at first. He was even standoffish. I think he may have disliked Letty's pushing me on him. But gradually he began to talk to me. And then one day he took me out to lunch. It seemed perfectly natural. Everyone in the office knows that Letty and I are best friends. She usually works at home, but she has an office at the magazine, of course, and never comes in without speaking to me. And after Eliot assigned me the job of helping him with the new column, we lunched together frequently to discuss it. And then . . . and then . . ." Her voice trailed off, and she ended with a shrug.

"Oh, Cora, how could you? With your dearest friend's husband?"

"Well, I did, Hubert." She wiped the sudden tears from her eyes and faced me. "You know how winning Eliot can be. And I'd never had a real lover in all my life! I tried to convince myself that Letty wouldn't care that much. I certainly resolved that she should never know. And if I helped myself to one little piece of happiness after all my years of frustration, was it really so wicked? Yes, I suppose it was."

"How did Ralph find out?"

"I don't know!" She gave a little cry of pain. "He must have been trailing me for weeks and hoping against hope that he'd catch me in something like this. And now I must accept his humiliating terms!"

"I'm afraid it's going to cost you a pretty penny."

"Anything is better than having Letty know! I couldn't bear to have Letty know that I'd betrayed her."

For a moment, I was rendered speechless by such a sacrifice. For even in a successful divorce for adultery, a husband might have to give his wife more than Ralph had offered.

"That's very big of you, my dear. I haven't a fortune, but what I have will always be at your disposal. And when I die I'll leave it to you. Alfreda and Letty will hardly need it."

Cora took my hand. "That's darling of you, Hubert. But don't forget. I still have my job. And Letty is very generous with her staff."

"Your job? You mean you'll go on with Eliot? After what's happened?"

"Certainly. We mustn't do anything to make Letty suspect."

"But you won't . . . ?" I couldn't finish.

"Carry on the affair? Oh, that's over and done with."

"How did that come about?"

"Because I found out that he didn't give a damn about me. I was only another tart to him. He had these terrible depressions when he would tell me that. And he was always ranting about Letty. He was obsessed with her!"

"You mean because he really cared for her, after all?"

"No! Because he really hates her!"

"Oh, my god! What makes you think that?"

"I feel it! He hates her because she owns all the things he thinks should be his. Because his successes are all really hers. Because she's *him!* And he was screwing me only to screw her. He's a fiend, Hubert!"

"Perhaps something simpler than that."

"Anyway, I'm terrified that in one of his blinding depressions he may tell Letty to get back at me for ending the affair. And to get back at her for being her. To destroy our friendship and knock her to bits. He'll tell her about Alfreda's baby, too."

"Oh, you know about that?"

"He told me. The man's capable of anything. Can't you do something about him, Hubert?"

"I can't think of what, but I can certainly try."

"If you think I should quit the magazine, I will."

"Certainly not. That's the one thing in your life that makes sense. Let's not throw everything away. But don't go to work today. Too much has happened. Why don't you go home now and have a nap and then meet me for lunch at Lutèce, where we'll talk only about pleasant things."

6.

In the first six years of their marriage, the Amorys seemed to be accomplishing everything that Elias Bernard had expected of their combined efforts. Eliot reduced his practice of law to a minimum, though retaining his partnership at a much smaller share of the firm profits, and devoted the bulk of his seemingly inexhaustible energies to the management of his late father-in-law's interests. He and Letty as coeditors of the magazine turned it into a major periodical of political and literary significance with a national circulation. Letty's securities swelled in value under Eliot's expert supervision, and the great ranch became a model for new techniques in the breeding and raising of cattle. With two fine little daughters, Letty and he appeared to be sitting on top of the world.

Did I ever think I had been wrong? Of course not. Alas, I had only apprehensively to wait.

———

Letty discovered an early infidelity of her husband's through a domestic incident overused in the trite chronicles of marital betrayal. Her shock and indignation were tempered with disgust at the banality of her experience. Checking the pockets of a jacket that Eliot had left on his bed for the cleaners, to be sure that no keys or other possessions had been carelessly forgotten, she had come across a scented epistle with an amatory greeting as crude as the letterhead was elegant. She did not hesitate to read it. It might almost have been placed there in order that she should do so. She had suspected such dalliances before, but had had no grounds for a spoken reproof. What should she do with such evidence? After much powerful cogitation, she decided to do nothing.

The first thing that struck her as she analyzed her reaction, with all the care and clarity of one who had devoted a quiet lifetime to the goals of objectivity and detachment, was that jealousy played the smallest part. She didn't give a damn about the woman who had written the letter—whom she easily identified as a researcher on the family foundation. She was quite able to recognize that her love for Eliot—if it really was love, and if not, what else was it?—was compatible with his taking an occasional roll in the hay. Suppose, for example, she had come into his bedroom and caught him masturbating? Ugh! But wasn't it basically the same thing? Didn't she share all that was best in Eliot: his brain, his ambition, his daughters, his everyday life? Or did she? Why should she feel that this letter in a jacket pocket was a long delayed challenge to the position she had so proudly taken as his partner? His *equal* partner. Ah, was that it?

So she did nothing, but she watched him much more closely than she had before. And in only a few weeks' time, she was startled to find that she was beginning to observe slight

changes in his appearance of which she had to have been pre-
viously aware but which she had presumably brushed aside
as irrelevant to herself and to her welfare. His waistline was
filling out, and his hair was faintly but noticeably receding.
He was still a fine-looking man, but he was not the apollo
she had once deemed him. All that, of course, was nothing,
but mightn't it somehow correlate with the increasingly au-
tocratic tone he was now taking at editorial meetings of the
magazine and the sharper note of his reproval at any defec-
tive service by their household staff?

She became even more acutely conscious of this at a meeting of the foundation to discuss a grant to a small and strug-
gling new art museum. Letty had wanted to make the gift
conditional on the widening of the extremely limited hours
of public admission that the donee, too intent, in her opinion, on access to scholars, was proposing.

"What is art if it's not *seen?*" she asked of her board. "This
business of restricting it to scholars obsessed with the concept of 'influence' can be overdone. We're always reading
about the influence of X on Y, of Monet on Manet, or money
on Monet, as if no great artist could ever think for himself!
And if it's not that, they're fixed on reattribution. I don't really give a damn if some kid in Rembrandt's studio painted
the *Polish Rider.* It's still a great picture. And all I want is to
look at it!"

"Letty, you're showing yourself a perfect philistine," Eliot
retorted testily. "How can you compare all those bleary-eyed
tourists who drag protesting children past masterpieces because they're told it's the thing to do with students willing to
give their very lives to the cause of art? What does the public learn by shuffling past great paintings? Can they tell the

difference between a sentimental daub by Bouguereau and a Madonna by Raphael? They might secretly prefer the former, but they're too awed by the critics to say so. Hang an old straw hat full of holes on the wall at the modern art museum and they'll respectfully gape!"

Letty had learned to be patient at such outbursts, which seemed to be increasing. "It's all very well for you to be snobbish, my dear," she replied. "But a foundation shouldn't be, and I'm afraid I'm not going to change my mind."

Eliot looked at her now with an expression she had never seen, at least as directed at her. She sensed something ominous in it. Where had she noticed it before? Was it when one of the editors of the magazine had effectively criticized a too violent column of his?

"Does that mean the grant will be disallowed if your condition is not met?" he demanded.

"I thought if either of us disagreed, that was enough to disallow it."

"You mean, darling, if *you* disagreed."

"Well, if it comes to that, we can recuse ourselves and leave the decision to the rest of the board."

"Knowing they will never go against the expressed opinion of the founder's heir and daughter!"

"You might dissuade them."

"Dream on. You know the board is your rubber stamp. I'm only sorry that you make it so clear."

"You will find, I think, Eliot, that your art scholars will do just as well with a larger public admitted to the galleries."

"You will always find what you want to find, my dear Letty. It's a way with heiresses."

The next time that Letty found an incriminating note in

a pocket of one of Eliot's jackets, she was sure that he had placed it there for her. She took it as his declaration of independence. For two years they had had separate bedrooms, as Eliot, an insomniac, had declined to bow to her objection to the reading light that he kept on till the early morning, but now he abandoned his occasional nocturnal visits to her chamber, and his demeanor, at meals and business meetings, was increasingly cool and distant.

At last they came to a decisive clash, and in the presence of the entire editorial board of the magazine. Eliot had requested that they hire a columnist who would chronicle the social side of life in Gotham: the big charity balls, the private lives of the politically and socially great, the rumors of coming events, even the scandals of notable folk.

"The little duc de Saint-Simon who was considered a minor snob and tattletale in his own day," he explained to the group, "is now revered as the primary source of our knowledge of the age of Louis XIV. What I am proposing is that we not wait a few centuries before drawing on the wealth of such a commentator but take advantage of it today. Great events often have their seed in matters that seemed trivial when they occurred. I see no reason why we should not sharpen our perceptions to avoid such misvaluations."

Letty had not come to the meeting unprepared. She had studied the work of the proposed columnist in another periodical and been appalled at what she had read. Her voice trembled slightly, but she was perfectly clear.

"The man is intelligent, undoubtedly," she conceded. "And he may be sincere in thinking that he is seeking the truth in his reports. But his glee in discovering scandal, his joy in dirt, betray a mind that is bent on dramatizing every bit of filth he can sniff out. That, to me, anyway, is not a voice we need to hear in the *New Orange*."

"Pardon me, Letitia. I had thought the *New Orange* was interested in facts. That a man takes pleasure in digging them out had not struck me as a disqualification. Perhaps *my* voice is the one that should not be heard in your chaste periodical."

Letty saw in the strained expressions of the four listening editors their concern over the bite in his tone. They all knew, as she did, that the issue was now joined, not only between owner and editor in chief, but between husband and wife. But it made her tone firmer.

"We need writers who would be just as glad to find the rumor of a scandal baseless as to find it authenticated. That is not true of your man."

"My man!"

"Your candidate, then."

"You mean that we should take a vote, the six of us?"

"We could start that way."

"And if the vote goes against you, you will exercise your veto?"

"If I see no other way to safeguard the integrity of the magazine."

"*The* magazine? You mean *your* magazine."

"If you must put it that way, yes."

"Is there any other way to put it?" Eliot rose now from his chair. "Gentlemen, I hereby resign my editorship. I leave you to your boss." And he strode quickly from the room.

"Let us call it a day, my friends," Letty said to the others. "Obviously, I have a lot to think over."

In the days that followed, Eliot refused even to speak to

Letty. He hung about the apartment, pale, tense, and moody. And then one morning after breakfasting alone, he departed, leaving a note instructing their housekeeper to send his clothes to his club. His two little daughters said nothing about all this. They were accustomed to their father's mood changes and frequent departures.

Letty had no idea as to what he would do next. She had long been used to his periodic depressions. It would not be wholly surprising if he suddenly returned, without a word of apology or explanation, and took up their life together as if nothing had happened. Or if, returning, he simply for a month or so remained sulkily in the apartment, silent, restless, unable to work, occasionally engaging in some mindless manual activity like polishing his leather-bound books with a special oil. But as his absence became prolonged without a word from him, she had to prepare herself for a graver course of conduct.

And then one morning a dreadful letter was hand delivered to her doorman.

"Like your father before you, you are a dangerous predator. You're like the desert wasp who devours the unconscious spider she has paralyzed with her sting. She can feed herself only with living flesh. I had the wit, the imagination, the genius you needed for your enterprises. I had to be caught, but I had to be caught alive. And now that I've begun to awaken, you have to sting me again. But you may not be able to catch me again. And watch out. The spider, now alert, may prove more than the equal of the wasp."

Letty wondered if he might not be suffering from a sort of dementia. There had been moments when she had been afraid that his depression might have pushed him temporarily over the edges of sanity. But before consulting a doctor, she decided to appeal to her old friend and mentor for guidance.

———

It was over a long lunch that Letty told me the sad story of Eliot's deterioration. She was fearsome that in one of his increasingly violent fits of manic depression he might actually do himself in. It seemed to me more likely that he would blurt out to the world—or to anyone who would listen—the sorry tale of how he had mistreated my three dear girls. Of course, there was always the hope that if he waxed mad enough, no one would believe him. But I could not persuade myself that Letty wouldn't believe him when he boasted what he had done with her two friends. There had to be some way to stop him.

After an afternoon of silent and solitary brooding on a Central Park bench, I decided to approach Eliot directly. He and I were both members of the Patroons Club, where I knew he was now staying, and at six o'clock I went to its bar, suspecting that he might be an early visitor. And indeed he came, before its usual customers, and, spotting me, he invited me—surprisingly—to join him at an unoccupied corner table. I could only surmise that he wanted to abuse poor Letty to me.

I was wrong. Sallow and yellow-looking, he seemed in the throes of a mood of neurotic self-reproach.

"You think I'm a cad, Hazelton, don't you? Of course you do. That's what you're thinking, isn't it? That I'm a stinking cad. And that I've always been one."

"I don't know about always," I responded dryly. "But you're certainly one now."

"And you despise me."

"I surely don't like you. You've been showered with every blessing a man could ask for. A loving wife, fine children, wealth, and even a bit of fame. And how have you thanked the gods who have so favored you? By spitting on their altars."

"Unlike you, is that right? Don't you call yourself *l'ami des femmes?*"

"Better than being their enemy."

"Is that what you're implying I am?"

"How else should I put it? Haven't you employed every resource of a twisted mind to ease their journey through life by removing every one of their cherished illusions?"

"Twisted mind?" His voice was suddenly grating. "Say what you will about my character, man, but leave my mind out of it."

"I believe my term is exact."

"Somebody's twisted, but is it me?" he sneered. "You call yourself women's friend, but why? Because you're incapable of being anything else. You haven't even the will to be the fag nature cut you out for. You're a friend of women because you're an old woman yourself."

"I'm glad you got that off your chest. I've always known it was there. We old bachelors have to live with that kind of aspersion. But now that you've cleared the air, would you like to hear what *your* relationship with women has been?"

"Very much. I'd like to hear it very much."

"Let us go back then to your premarital days. I well recall what a cheerful young apollo you were. Oh, so bright and shining! But there was something just a bit off—a wee bit off. You smiled too much. The late Mr. Bernard himself once pointed that out. You wanted the whole world, but you were not convinced that you had all the means and talent needed to get it. You had a lot, to be sure, but the world was a big thing. So your smile would be your excuse if you failed. So long as you smiled people wouldn't think you took yourself too seriously. And if you didn't take yourself too seriously, could it be said that you had really failed? Could it even be said that you had really tried? Your face would have been saved, and a very handsome face it was."

I paused, but he simply said, "Go on."

"At last, you looked about to see who could supply you with what you lacked. Who was more obvious than Mr. Bernard? He had everything you wanted, everything you needed, plus a rather plain daughter to whom he would leave it all and whom Apollo could easily captivate. It was ABC, the old American story, and it worked like the proverbial charm. Everything fell plumb into your lap. But there was a catch. Letty not only had the material things with which you had not been endowed; she had all the brains and the guts that you lacked. Where you were all show and glitter, she was the solid rock beneath. It was she who was the real voice on the magazine, the ranch, and the foundation. You thought you had acquired her. She had acquired you! You were the tinsel she had needed for her Yuletide tree!"

Amory gave vent to a snotty laugh. "Now I see why fags make such good novelists! Proust and James. You should have written fiction, Hazelton. You've wasted your silly life."

But I could read the real anger in his narrowed eyes. I had struck home.

"Your story wouldn't make a novel, Amory," I retorted. "No one would believe it. It's interesting only because it's true, and truth is not the staple of fiction, which, unlike life, must have probability."

"Go on, anyway, with your crazy tale. I want to hear how it comes out."

"You will, Amory. You will. Well, the next thing that you find is that Letty always gets her own way, not yours. You very much wanted a son to bolster you against your dominating spouse, and what did she produce but two females, before having to give up any further idea of childbirth? Siegfried would find himself surrounded by the Valkyries that his Wotan father-in-law had engendered. What next? You had been Alfreda Newbold's confidant in her plan to have what she was oddly confident would be a son. You would sire a male child on the body of your wife's best friend! What finer triumph could a frustrated husband have?"

Eliot's anger was almost smothered in his obvious astonishment. "So you knew about me and Alfreda?"

"Of course I knew. My girls tell me everything. And I made her feel thoroughly ashamed of what she had done and promise that she would never let on to anybody how the child was conceived. I knew that would keep you silent, too, for how would you look boasting about a thing that Alfreda would surely deny? Your only further revenge on the women in your wife's life who had given her the affection that you hadn't would now be to debauch the second of Letty's two friends, Cora, taking advantage of the poor woman's unhappy marriage. What a stud! Are congratulations in order?" And I mockingly raised my glass.

But Amory made no answering gesture or retort. He simply lapsed into a moody silence, as I sat there, watching him. Finally he signaled a waiter and ordered a double brandy.

When it came, he drank it off in a few gulps, still without a word. When he spoke, it was in an untypically subdued tone.

"I suppose you are, in your own mad way, a friend of women. What will you do for your sacred trio now?"

"Nothing at present. But I can tell you what you can do for them."

"Supposing that I want to?"

"Well, yes, supposing that. Not that you do. But, anyway, you might take yourself to the top of a high building and jump off."

Amory threw back his head and laughed, almost raucously. "Hubert, I love you!" he cried. "They broke the mold when they made you." He rose. "Good night."

The next morning the chambermaid who came to make up his bed found him dead in it. He had swallowed a lethal dose of sleeping pills. Nobody has ever learned or even suspected the gist of our final conversation, though one member of the club, who had observed us in our corner, asked me if I had any clue as to why he had taken his life. I told him I hadn't. So what I said to Amory that evening stands alone and stark before myself as both judge and jury.

Was I guilty of manslaughter or even murder in having so excoriated a man locked in the dark prison of mental aberration? Morally, perhaps so. But I am unrepentant. I am convinced that he would have got better only to get worse, and that he would have brought even more misery than he desired to my girls. Letty without him has gone on to become one of the nation's leading editors. Cora is now a popular columnist on a big daily paper. And Alfreda has raised a splendid son who is the apple of her husband's eye. I think I can almost justify my self-imposed title of *l'ami des femmes*.

THE DEVIL AND
RUFUS LOCKWOOD

BEFORE I WAS ORDAINED a priest of the Episcopal Church and while I was still in divinity school, I became something of a specialist in the early history of Christianity, and it seems now appropriate, or perhaps even essential, in this year of our Lord 1937, and in the wasteland that my life has already become at the age of only thirty, to adopt some form of confession, as did many of the early desert fathers in their wrestling with God. I pray that it may bring me back to Him, from whom I appear to have been alienated. Since my resignation of the chaplaincy of Averhill School last year, I have done little but mope and worry in our tiny Boston flat until poor Hilda, my much put-upon wife, has besought me to seek enough financial aid from the church to send me for a time at least to a sanitarium. But let me try confession first.

I was born in Ayer, Massachusetts, the youngest, smallest, and by far the least strapping of a family that had produced three Dartmouth football stars in my three elder brothers. My father, a lawyer with a modest small-town general practice, died when I was five, and my mother, a stalwart and heroic woman, managed on a tight budget to raise and educate her brood with such success that my brothers in time became prosperous professional men—a surgeon, an accountant, and another lawyer. I was her single failure, at least until I began to grow a bit in mind and body at divinity school. Before then I had been hopeless in sports, poor in grades, and unpopular with my peers. My mother and brothers had always been moderately kind to me, but I was ever conscious of the condescension and disappointment behind their perfunctory encouragement. I had really only God to appeal to, for I was always intensely religious—what else had I?—until Hilda came to supplement the deity.

She was an Ayer neighbor, a Vassar girl who loved poetry and hoped to write it; she was, like me, small, and, yes, I can say it, a touch on the plain side, but she also had the brave soul of a missionary, and she took it into her head early that she could make something of me. Could she succeed where my redoubtable mother could not? She thought so, anyway, and by the time we were secretly engaged, I was already enrolled at Harvard Divinity School. She had convinced me that I was cut out to be a priest and had pried out of my doubting mother the funds for my tuition.

It was as a divinity student that I became interested—perhaps too intensely so—in the first three centuries of the Christian era, when it was torn by bitter conflicts between the different sects that bloomed like mushrooms in that primitive soil. I was fascinated by the variegated dogmas of religious dissent and spent so much time analyzing the distinctions between them that one of my teachers subjected me to a gentle reproach.

"It will not be necessary, Percy Goodheart, for you as a pastor to instruct your flock in these ancient heresies. They are forgotten now except by the more erudite scholars. You would do better to concentrate on the church after it was united in faith by such councils as that of Nicaea."

This was true enough, but two hard questions continued to aggravate me. My teacher had spoken of the church as united, but could we Episcopalians see much truth in that? Had our forebears not split off from Catholic Rome, and were there not dozens of Protestant denominations today? And more every decade? And had not these alien sects had their own martyrs? Had so-called heretics not shared death in the arena with the orthodox? So that even a ghastly demise might not prove truth.

The question of whether it was ever required by God to suffer death for His sake haunted me. I was terribly afraid that I would have funked it before the Roman police and abjured my faith. But would God have really cared so long as I retained it in my heart and mind, and saved my life to serve Him? This idea drew me to the Gnostics, who had made the same argument, affirming that if the spirit was all and the body nothing, it could hardly matter whether the body was tortured or not. And I was also attracted to their belief that the archons of the cruel Jewish deity of the Old Testament had held captive the spirit of man until the aeon Jesus had been sent to restore him to the divine knowledge, or gnosis.

Similarly, Manichaeism had its lure. That the dualism that we sense in things around us may be true I could well imagine, for evil seemed quite as real to me as good. Manichaeans maintained that it was only matter that was bad: man did not suffer from the Fall but from his contact with matter—Eve ate of the apple. The asceticism, even the celibacy of this faith appealed to me. Had I not seen what the lust in my brothers' big strong bodies had led them to, at least before they were happily chained in lawful wedlock? Was not the very weakness of my own physique evidence of my greater freedom from matter and even the probable cause of my being so able and willing to dedicate myself to holy orders? I love Hilda, of course, but our love was chaste, and we did not become one flesh until we were married.

I also saw much to reflect upon in Arianism. Isn't there more than a bit of that heresy in even the most orthodox of Episcopalians? When we think of a triune god, aren't we thinking of three distinct deities? And didn't the Arians have a point when they insisted that the Son had to have been born *after* the Father and therefore, if coexistent, couldn't be coeternal?

The doubts that these speculations aroused in my troubled psyche at length engendered grave misgivings as to whether I was qualified to be a minister, and eventually I found myself on the verge of a nervous breakdown. I don't know what would have happened to me had not Hilda, my patient but sorely tried fiancée, who was always urging me to concentrate more on the ecclesiastical present than its past, finally persuaded me to lay my problem before the dean. That great wise and good man at once took me under his wing and straightened me out, to the extent, anyway, of my finishing school and becoming ordained. I recall what he said about the essence of evil.

"You mustn't be obsessed by it, Percy. We all know there's plenty of it around for us to deal with, without wasting our days and nights philosophizing about its nature or origin. We know what atrocities are going on in the world; we need look no further than the Spanish civil war. You wonder why Christians once killed one another over creeds and why God allowed it. Because, as Saint Thomas Aquinas said, He gave us free will, and some men are bound to abuse the privilege.

Would you rather He had made us robots? And don't worry about hell, dear boy. There may be punishment in another life, but it cannot be eternal, for how could we be happy in heaven knowing that persons whom we perhaps may have loved were condemned to eternal torment?"

Thanks to this beneficent gentleman I was able, with Hilda, whom I married the very day after my ordainment, to undertake the pastorship of a small rural Massachusetts diocese in the neighborhood of the fashionable Averhill, a boarding school for boys. We were very happy there for a couple of years—somewhat innocently happy, as it now seems to me. I was able to get on with, and even to be liked by, my simple congregation of farmers and village storekeepers, and I hope that I offered them some spiritual edification. Hilda enjoyed her neighborhood visits to parishioners who were sick or lonely or in need of some consolation, and she had ample time for her poetry. In due course a dear little girl was born to us. All seemed well.

Then fate intervened. Out of neighborly courtesy, the famous veteran headmaster of Averhill, the Reverend Rufus Lockwood, invited me to preach at the school chapel on a Sunday when he and his chaplain were to be at some ecclesiastical conference. It so happened that the sudden illness of Mrs. Lockwood—at first seemingly dangerous but soon proved innocuous—brought her husband home prematurely, and he found it possible to come to the service in time to hear my sermon. Fortunately (or perhaps unfortunately, as things turned out) it was one of my best, in which I offered the proposition that God did not expect us all to be martyrs or heroes and that even those who led the most ordinary and routine of lives were equal to the saints in His eyes if they were true to His precepts. A week later Dr. Lockwood invited me to lunch with him in the headmaster's house, during which he questioned me in depth about my life and projects. It is notable that he never bothered to explain to me what right or reason he had to put me through such an examination. Before that gruff and stolid inquirer I might have been just another of his students, subjected to some disciplinary interrogation. Yet I found myself as submissive as one of his boys. The man certainly had what I believe is known in military circles as command presence.

It appeared that his chaplain had received a sudden and challenging calling from a parish in the South, and Lockwood had to find his replacement by the start of the next school year. It was now May.

Lockwood, as I soon realized to be his habit, made up his mind quickly, and I received his offer at the end of our meal. I pointed out that I could hardly leave my parish on such short notice.

"Leave that to me" was his abrupt response. "I'll speak to the bishop."

Hilda was excited by the prospect. Averhill was a famous school; it promised a bigger life. She brought up that it was a miraculous chance for a couple as obscure as ourselves and might never come again. When the bishop himself called me to stress the importance to the church of getting immediate support for an aging cleric as nationally known as Dr. Lockwood, my last misgivings about abandoning my dear parishioners were quashed.

And so my life at Averhill commenced. Let me start by describing the headmaster, for he was everything at that school. He had founded it as a young man, developed it from an academy of twenty pupils to one of five hundred, and had ruled over it for almost a half century. To put it simply, he *was* Averhill.

Just to look at him was to receive an impression of craggy strength. At seventy-eight he was short but stoutly built, with a plain square face, a gleaming balding pate, and large, staring green-blue eyes. His voice was like that of an old repertory actor: it could sink to a velvety softness or crescendo into a lion's roar. He came of common stock, reputedly the son of a butcher, and had the strength associated with that calling.

He had fought his way up the social ladder to the ministry and married a Boston Lowell. He reigned in Averhill like a despot, mostly, it was at least supposed, as a benevolent one. The boys were in awe of him; the faculty bowed to him; the trustees were his rubber stamp. It was rumored that when one of the latter had uttered something about retirement, Lockwood had gazed down the table and simply murmured, "I must be getting deaf—I thought I heard someone suggest that I should step down." This was followed by a shocked silence, as all glared at the offending trustee. Even the parents, including the many fathers who were themselves alumni, hardly dared question his decrees. Only Mrs. Lockwood could oppose him, and she was largely preoccupied with charitable work in the neighborhood. But on the rare occasions when she did, he was the butcher's son before a Brahmin.

The school now boasted a magnificent campus of semi-Palladian buidings around a huge circular lawn dominated by a Richardsonian chapel as craggy as the headmaster and a splendid gymnasium designed by Frank Lloyd Wright. To pay for it all, Lockwood had twisted the arms of a multitude of tycoons, not ever bothering, it was said, to investigate the tainted sources of some of the fortunes he tapped. However a muscular Christian he proclaimed himself to be, the principle that the end justifies the means must have been engraved on his heart.

There had even been, at least in the past, a good deal of gossip about his obsequious kowtowing to wealthy parents and alumni, his admitting some unqualified progeny of theirs to the ranks of his students, his support of a notoriously crooked Massachusetts politician who had taken the school's side in a suit with the state, and his retainer of shyster lawyers who defended Averhill's wobbly case in a bitter dispute with a neighboring town. But by the time I came to be his chaplain, all his fights had been won, and his reputation as a great teacher and silver-tongued orator had silenced dissent. When he raised his voice in passionate prayer in chapel, it seemed impossible that he was not being heard on high.

I pause as I read the last sentence. Is there a note of levity in it? Have I taken from Lockwood himself the scurrilous habit of seeming almost to mock the very faith that is my mainstay? I must, however, as a part of this confession (or self-probing, whichever and whatever it may be), make explicit just what it was that troubled me most in my relationship with him. He seemed at once a Dr. Jekyll and a Mr. Hyde. Which role was he acting? Both?

For in chapel, and in serious talks to the boys in his study, he was very open and articulate in the pronouncement of his faith. He spoke of God as if He were always present, always with us, in our most public or most private moments; Lockwood made one feel that God could be told anything, even one's most disgusting fantasies. And it was obvious that many boys were inspired by him. In every sixth form, some became almost troublesomely devout and cultivated the headmaster's company like so many disciples.

Yet all this was in constant contrast to his iron rule, the harshness of some of his punishments, his habit of raucously laughing at anything that smacked of a pathetic ignorance or a too prim propriety, his savage jokes and take-offs, his occasional monumental shrug at some of the very precepts he enforced. He could be, when the mood seized him, the bluff actor who cried, "All the world's a stage!" There were moments when I seemed to see a devil hiding behind him. Which of us was crazy?

My job, formally, was to assist him in chapel services, to conduct them in his absence, and to teach sacred studies to the younger classes. But these relatively simple tasks paled beside the much more arduous one of being a kind of personal assistant to the headmaster, drafting his letters to parents, donors, and other school heads, checking references in his sermons and public addresses, carrying messages to staff members he was sometimes too busy to see, touring the school grounds to inspect reported malfunctions of the infrastructure, and at times even acting as a valet, robing him in chapel, driving him to Boston if his chauffeur was indisposed, and assisting Mrs. Lockwood on "parlor night," when certain privileged boys were invited to her house for games.

It was tiring work, for Lockwood was always unpredictable. I never knew when he was going to be gravely impassive, as if I were not even present, or when he would shout at me and call me an ass, or when, if my little daughter was ailing, he would be wonderfully sympathetic, almost paternal. It was again the repertory: Tamburlaine one day, Falstaff the next.

One thing, however, was certain. He was always observant; he missed nothing. He spotted all my vulnerabilities,
and he could play with me as a cat does with a mouse. There
must have been a touch of sadism in his makeup. Why should
he, a great man, take any notice at all of such a microbe as
myself? Because he couldn't keep his hands off anything
within his reach. He always had to be creating something of
something.

My real trouble was with Hilda. She was soon disillu-
sioned with the life of a master's wife, particularly a master
so low in the faculty ratings at Averhill. She found the other
wives, all considerably older than she, both dull and condescending, and there was little for her to do. In my parish she
had had the sick and senile to call upon, and others in for
tea, but Averhill operated perfectly without her, and she had
no duties but to sit on my right at a long table of boys in the
big dining hall for Sunday lunch. But worst of all were the
constant inroads into our domestic life made by the ever demanding headmaster. He would telephone at all hours, usually with some peremptory demand that I come straight over
to him, and not hesitate to make hash of any little plans Hilda
and I might have had for our theoretical free time, such as
playing bridge with neighbors or going to a movie. And it
galled poor Hilda that I was so submissive; she accused me
of lying supine before him, which I'm afraid I did. But then
it has never been in my nature to assert myself; I have always
bowed to authority.

"You're under his spell!" she warned me. "The devil himself is in that man! I actually believe he's trying to take you
from me!"

"Why would he want such a poor thing as myself?"

"Do devils need motives? They collect souls. Even poor souls!"

Of course, Hilda didn't really mean what she said, but the unfortunate (or fortunate?) result of her colorful imagery was that it stirred up all my old divinity school speculations on early Christian heresies and, in particular, the stubborn clinging of some dissidents to the notion that if good is real, so must be evil. They had argued that, as it seems impossible that a benevolent deity could have created evil, it must have come into being on its own, and it must therefore oppose God with an independent identity. If we posit God, must we not do the same for Satan? Did I really believe this? Do I now? How much of the truth, anyway, do we know?

As it happened, the day after Hilda had put the idea of the devil in my turbid mind, I was standing behind the headmaster after the Sunday service in the garth by the chapel, where he received the visiting alumni and parents who had lined up to greet him and compliment him on his sermon. But when he spied a little old brown-clad woman in the crowd, a humble contrast to the smartly dressed mothers, he hurried over to her with outstretched arms, exclaiming, "Oh, Mrs. Tomkins, I'm so happy to see you up and around after your bout with flu. Come, let me introduce you to some of our illustrious trustees who have come up for a board meeting."

Now, I knew that Mrs. Tomkins, a simple farmer's widow of small means, happened to be one of the handful of members of the tiny parish comprising the Averhill grounds, and that she was not connected in any way with the school. Lockwood was demonstrating to the crowd that he was not above giving to the few poor and lowly under his care the same attention that, as a headmaster, he accorded to those of his institution. Poor Mrs. Tomkins, who wanted only to take herself home, had to have her thin fingers squeezed in the firm grasp of stalwart moguls. It was Lockwood the repertory actor again. I was put in mind of the scene in *Richard III* where the duke of Gloucester, anxious to impress upon the visiting mayor of London and his suite that he has no wicked designs on the crown, parades piously before them, arm in arm with two bishops, an open prayer book in one hand, apparently oblivious to everything but his contemplation of God.

I was startled, the following Monday, as I was preparing in my classroom for the approaching hour of sacred studies, to receive a visit from Lockwood, who wanted to discuss the very heresies that had recurred to my mind. I had even forgotten that I had once asked his opinion on Gnosticism. Needless to say, he never forgot anything.

"I think, Goodheart, that you might share some of your expertise on the early church with your students."

"But am I not to confine myself to *sacred* studies, sir?"

"Early divisions in the flock can be a part of that. No boy can fully understand the history of Christianity by reading only of martyrs consumed by lions. He should see it from different points of view. Like Renan's or Strauss's. They saw Jesus as a barely educated thaumaturge with a remarkable gift for words and a high standard of ethics, who urged his followers to submit to the harshness of Roman rule and all the injustices of life in order to prepare themselves for the Judgment Day that would, in a few years' time, put an end to the world. What was the point of fussing about anything else in view of the imminent dissolution? But when the early church was faced not only with the fact that the Day of Judgment seemed indefinitely postponed, but that the faith was being rent by dissention, it had to unite the sects under a new set of dogmas and prepare to rule the world!"

"But Renan and Strauss, sir, denied the divinity of Christ!"

"Of course I know that."

"And isn't that the essence of our faith? Isn't that what I have to teach the boys?"

"Have I said otherwise? But you can also teach them what so many other people have thought. At the least it is interesting, and sacred studies notoriously bores boys. You can see their heads straighten up the moment you mention a controversy."

"I'll try, sir."

"See that you do, Goodheart. I'll audit your class in a week or so."

But could it possibly be right to introduce a topic that might cause a sensitive boy some of the anguished doubt that it had in my own earlier being? What could be the headmaster's motive in directing my teaching down this troublesome course? Was it conceivable that some malign force in the old man's subconscious was working to undermine the very institution that he would have sold his soul to create?

It was all very well for me to try to laugh myself out of any such arcane and bizarre theories, but a subsequent discussion with Lockwood in his office brought them back violently to mind. He had asked me to draft a letter to a trustee explaining why he could not honor the latter's request that a Jewish boy be admitted to the school.

"The boy has a first-class record in his high school," I felt obliged, however timidly, to point out.

"But he's Jewish, Goodheart! What are you talking about? Are we a church school or are we not?"

"But exposed to our church, sir, might he not come to see the light? It's odd enough that his orthodox parents should be willing to send him here. Mightn't that be a sign that it's our mission to help the boy?"

"A sign that you're an ass, my dear fellow!"

"But we have the Kramer boys and the Streyers."

"They're Episcopalians!"

"They're still Jewish, sir."

"Racially, of course. But a converted Jew is a Christian, is he not? I know we have parents who insist that he's not, that is, if he converted for reasons of social advancement. But why are many Christians Christians, but for social advancement or, at least, social acceptance? We don't have to go into that. We might not like what we find. I can't blame a Jew who abandons his old faith. The god of the Old Testament is a terrible deity who slays all who fail to worship him and many who don't. Even if our Christian faith is an illusion, I still cling to it."

"Surely you don't ever believe it's an illusion, sir?"

His answer was a roar. "Don't tell me what I believe or don't believe, Goodheart!"

His anger at last stirred whatever bit of man there was in me. Had I not the cross of Christ behind me? "No, sir. But you have Catholic boys in the school. And Catholic boys who have no idea of converting."

"But their god is close to ours. Perhaps the same. And we all might still be Catholics if Anne Boleyn hadn't refused to spread her legs until the lecherous Harry promised her a wedding ring."

I was visibly shocked. "Oh, sir!"

"Oh, sir!" he repeated mockingly. "Listen to me, my boy, for you're not a bad preacher, and I may make something of you yet. This thing we're discussing is an excellent example of how a headmaster can keep a school both successful in a worldly sense and decent, to boot. How, if you want to put it that way, he can have his cake and eat it. To begin with, I cannot afford totally to ignore the prejudice that many of our parents have about not wishing their sons to be brought up cheek by jowl with Jewish boys. So I compromise. I rule that there will be no place for an orthodox Jew in a church school. But if he's converted, I take him. Oh, yes, there are some parents who will still growl, but they know, fundamentally, that they don't have a leg to stand on, and I have shown myself a consistent man of principle. Do you get it now?"

"But the Catholic boys don't have to convert."

"Ah, you spy an inconsistency. Life is full of them. Let me point out that our parents and alumni may have a prejudice against Catholicism but not against Catholics themselves. They have no objection to having their sons raised with Catholic boys so long as Catholicism is not taught or advocated in the school. So what do I do? I require that Catholic students attend all our chapel services but send them to Mass in the village in a bus."

"Mightn't an orthodox Jewish boy accept the same treatment? And go to the temple in a bus?"

"As Lewis Carroll's Father William put it, I have answered three questions, and that is enough. Be off or I'll kick you downstairs!"

But I left him wondering if being kicked downstairs was enough. Mightn't it be better if I was kicked out of the school? Hadn't I had a glimpse of the complete amorality of this supposedly devout Christian? Hadn't he sufficiently demonstrated that, if he had no prejudices, neither did he have any convictions, and that he would go to any lengths, perhaps even improper, to promote the worldly prosperity of the academy to which he had dedicated his life? He might fool everyone else, but could he fool God? Or was it that he was sparring with God? Challenging God on seemingly equal terms with sword drawn? Ah, Satan! Wasn't Satan as real as God?

That night I had a grim nightmare. As often takes place in my dreams, I was an anchorite living in a community of mud huts in a North African desert in early Christian times. I was seeking, as usual, peace of the soul, communion with God, and had little difficulty resisting the lewd temptations of the imps who danced around the pious village, hoping to lure one or another of its inmates to the fleshpots of the nearest city. I was wholly intent on the wise and comfortable words of the old abbot who was our self-constituted leader. He appeared as none other than Dr. Lockwood himself, though not the arbitrary and formidable headmaster I saw in the schoolroom, but the gentler cleric I sometimes saw in chapel when his velvet tones swelled to plangent oratory in the pulpit or when he knelt in prayer, his eyes tightly closed, his hands clasped, his voice trembling in a kind of pious ecstasy.

What turned this placid dream into a nightmare was my happening to see, when I was passing his hut at dusk and he was unaware of my proximity, that he was addressing a respectful half-circle of imps seated quietly at his feet and evidently receiving his instruction!

I sat up with a cry that awakened Hilda, to whom I related

my dream. Ordinarily I shouldn't have done this, for she had little patience with my nocturnal fantasies, but in my dismay I blurted it all out. She simply laughed.

"So that's how you see him edifying his sacred school! Well, all I can say is that I wouldn't put anything past him."

A week later Hilda, as with her basic kindness she sometimes did, invited Miss Ethelinda Snyder, a small, giggling, and gossip-loving old maid, to supper with us. She was Dr. Lockwood's secretary and, of course, his awestricken slave. Yet his treatment of her, unlike his of me, was always kind and courteous; he could afford to shed his benignity on creatures in whom the least spark of independence had been effectively quashed. The poor woman had little or no social life, as the faculty wives had no use for her and the local villagers never cultivated the school staff. She was enchanted to come to us when asked and partook a bit too freely of the sherry I offered her.

On one such visit the three of us happened to be discussing the approaching end-of-year departure of a history teacher who had accepted what he evidently considered a better offer to teach at Groton. Miss Snyder hinted darkly that it was just as well that he had decided to go.

"Why is that?" I asked. "Was Mr. Higgins in some kind of trouble here?"

Miss Snyder looked cryptic. "Well, I shouldn't say anything, but . . ." She paused.

"Oh, come on, Ethelinda," my wife intervened. "You know how discreet Percy and I are. And we're dying for some juicy tidbit to liven up our dull lives. Don't be stuffy."

"Well, I happen to know that Dr. Lockwood had a letter from the father of a fifth former complaining that Mr. Higgins had written his son a letter in the summer vacation that the father considered to be couched in rather too affectionate terms."

"If Lockwood kicks out every master who's done *that*," Hilda asserted roundly, "he may have to get a new faculty."

"But that's the way he is," Miss Snyder said hurriedly. "He's death on that subject. So when the letter from Groton came, he passed it right on to Mr. Higgins."

"Didn't he have to do that anyway?" I demanded in some surprise. "Why didn't Groton write directly to Higgins?"

"Oh, that's not the etiquette," Miss Snyder explained. "If you want a teacher from another school, you write first to his headmaster." She giggled. "And you won't be too surprised, I'm sure, to learn that some of those letters stick to Dr. Lockwood's desk."

"You mean he doesn't forward them?"

"I mean nothing else. Dr. Lockwood doesn't hesitate to take on himself the decision to sit on letters which might result in his losing a teacher he thinks valuable to the school."

Miss Snyder looked at us here with a sly wink. She evidently loved showing her intimate knowledge of the habits of the great. The sherry was doing its work.

"But what would he say to the headmaster making the offer?"

"Oh, he would simply write that the teacher whom the other school wanted was happy at Averhill."

"Ethelinda, you're fantasizing!"

"What makes you so sure of that, Percy?" my wife now indignantly injected. "Really, your subservience to that old slave driver is becoming obsessive. If you were a black, I'd call you an Uncle Tom!"

"But, Hilda, Ethelinda doesn't seem to realize what she's saying!" I was really hot now. "It's one thing to call a man a slave driver. It's quite another to call him a crook. To accuse him of telling lies in order to cheat an employee out of the chance to better himself! Think of it! It's preposterous!"

Miss Snyder was now aroused to defend her veracity at any cost. Her cheeks were dyed a mottled red. "How would you like to know what happened in your own case, Percy Goodheart? You, who seem to know everything? Did I not myself type a letter to Dr. Cram of the Derby School explaining that you were too happy with your position at Averhill to ever think of leaving?"

"Oh, my god!" This was from Hilda. "That must have been what my friend Anita Hunt was hinting at! Her husband is a master at Derby, and she told me he had suggested to the headmaster that Percy might be a possibility as head of the lower school!"

Miss Snyder, realizing now the full extent of her indiscretion, implored me not to betray her. She waxed almost hysterical, crying, "I'll lose my job! I'll lose everything I've got. Oh, please, dear Percy, don't say anything about this. After all, it shows how much Dr. Lockwood esteems you. You know he'd do anything for the school. And Derby's not all that great, anyway. It's not half the size of Averhill!"

I finally quieted her down, gave her an aspirin and a dose of whiskey, and walked her to her tiny cottage in the village. When I returned, I found Hilda with a dark drink, looking ominous.

"I hope this will finally pull the scales off your eyes, Percy. I trust you will now see how tightly the old devil has you in his clutches. And I'm going to drive over to Derby and talk to

Anita and see if that job might still be open. Anything to get us out of here!"

I told her there would be no use in that. I had already learned from other sources that Anita's husband himself had been given the post. And I wasn't even sure that I would have taken it if it had been directly offered. But I didn't wish to discuss my more somber suspicions about Lockwood's conduct. I was almost frightened myself by them, and I knew she would simply think I was crazy.

We were both exhausted when we finally went to bed, and I was still in a comalike sleep when the harsh jangle of the bedside telephone awoke me at six. Hilda answered, and I heard the headmaster's peremptory "Put Percy on, please." She handed me the phone without comment. Lockwood told me gruffly to change the hymn for morning chapel from the one assigned to "Oh, Jesus, art Thou standing, outside the fast-closed door?" and hung up.

That morning in his office he brought up a dormitory master's discovery of some sexual activity among certain boys at night. The supposed ringleader had been sent home, and I was to see what personal possessions the boy had left at school.

Armed with Miss Snyder's revelation, I found myself able for once to voice a query. "Is what the boy did, sir, really grounds for expelling him? I'm not defending it, certainly, but I'm afraid it's not uncommon with juveniles. We know, for example, that at St. Jude's last year—"

"I'm not expelling him," Lockwood interrupted. "And I don't give a tinker's damn what happened at St. Jude's. Expelling him would be to make this thing public and give us a bad name. Bigger and bugger things at Averhill! Can't you hear them?"

I looked down at my knees in embarrassment. "But if you say he's not coming back, sir?"

"He's not. His father agreed to withdraw him. On grounds of health. It appears the poor fellow has asthma."

Had he actually winked at me? It was hard to tell. "Then the father knows the real reason?"

"Of course he knows. I made it very clear."

"Mightn't he be too shocked? Mightn't he take it out on the boy?"

"That's no concern of mine. The welfare of the school is my concern. This way the whole matter will be swept under the rug, which is where it belongs. You will find that rugs have their uses, my friend. The father will never tell. It's not something he's likely to boast about. And the boys here will all know why Hudgins isn't coming back and will be much more discreet in the future."

"Discreet?"

"Yes. If a boy learns not to do openly what he can be punished for, he will have learned a valuable lesson in life."

"But he can do it in private? Or in vacations from school?"

"I didn't say that, Goodheart. Don't put words in my mouth."

"But, sir, I'm a priest! There are things I must ask!"

"Does being a priest involve butting in where you're not wanted? Well, perhaps that *is* what being a priest involves. Go ahead then. Ask your question."

"Did you mean to imply, sir, that what Hudgins did was not wrong in itself?"

"And if I did?"

"Then, sir, isn't he being wrongfully punished?"

"For doing something that may give the school a bad name? Hardly."

"Oh, sir, can that be right?"

"Goodheart, there are moments when I wonder if I will ever succeed in making a man of you. The purpose of Averhill is to train youths to become leaders in *this* world, not in some utopia of your dreams. And you're not going to become a leader if you go about outraging a possible majority of humans who cling, however blindly, to their inherited prejudices. Except, of course, when a real moral issue is at stake."

"And when is that?"

"What the Nazis in Germany are doing to the Jews is one. That must be resisted to the death. But what is not one is the whole question of sexual deviation. There are activities which one can condone if they are decently concealed. I happen, for example, to know that one of the great benefactors of this school is a homosexual. He has a wife and children and leads a life of the utmost respectability, yet I have reason to believe that he is a regular visitor to a male brothel. What's that to me? Nothing!"

"And what is it to God?"

"Oh, Goodheart, get out of here. And bring me your notes for my graduation address at noon."

It was at this point that I began to understand that Lockwood had built his school as the Christian Church had been built in the age of Constantine. Anything was permissible that would hammer in the nails that were to support the steel edifice that was to dominate the world of believers. The meekness and humility of Jesus's teaching was muted; the simplicity and gentleness of the early fathers was forgotten; a new theology was constructed; dissent was crushed. The warrior priest replaced the martyr. Salvation could be attained only through the church militant.

The foe to be suppressed was no longer Rome. Rome had been taken over, and the Inquisition would one day replace the Praetorian Guard. The real foe was to be found in heresies: in Manichaeism, in Gnosticism, in Arianism. They were the heralds of Antichrist. But didn't the heretics see Antichrist in the church itself? And mightn't I see a devil in Rufus Lockwood?

I do not know what would have emerged from my seething doubts and troubles had it not been for the case of Nicholas Rice. He was an Averhill graduate who had left before my time and whose wealthy father, Lyman Rice, was still the chairman of the school's board of trustees. Nicholas had been known while at Averhill to be a deeply serious and religious boy and one of the headmaster's special favorites, a "disciple," as he had liked to call himself. But at Harvard he had become a Catholic convert, despite his having surprised his friends by turning into a high-living epicurean, and after graduation he had put the cap on a variegated career by entering a Trappist monastery. This last twist had just happened and was the talk of the Averhill campus. The story that went around was that on the very eve of taking his final vows, he hosted a drunken and raucous party for his bachelor friends in a private dining room at his club.

The headmaster said nothing about it, and my curiosity—for it was impossible that he shouldn't have been concerned—gave me the nerve to make this comment at one of our daily meetings in his office.

"It must be so hard on his father," I ventured.

"Yes, Lyman has taken it very hard," Lockwood answered,

shaking his head and frowning. "It has almost killed the poor man. He's a loving parent but not one to let his son live his own life. Few fathers do."

Lockwood had no children himself, and I would not have guaranteed their independence if he had. "Perhaps his son may come back to him yet," I surmised. "That wild party on the eve of his vow taking doesn't sound like the affair of a man who will submit forever to a monastic regime."

"Oh, Nick knows what he's doing," Lockwood affirmed gravely. "He'll stay the course. And I think that farewell party had a certain style to it. You didn't know Nick, but he has style. He could pick up a glass of gin and stare at it and say slowly to himself, 'This is the last glass of gin I'll ever drink'—and mean it." Here Lockwood picked up the water glass on his desk and held it in front of him, staring at it intently. After a moment he put it down.

"How tragic, then," I exclaimed, "that a young man of such spirit should wall himself up in a monastery and be lost to any useful function in life!"

Lockwood's gaze was stern. "Who is to say he's lost? Have you penetrated all the mysteries of life, Goodheart?"

"Hardly. But you yourself, sir, must regret that so promising a graduate of yours should be lost to his family and friends. And lost to the great career he might have had and to the woman he might have married. And to our church, sir. Lost to our church!"

"He made the decision that, after long consideration, he thought best for himself. I know how deeply he thought about it, for he honored me by consulting me over each step that he took."

"But surely, sir, you never encouraged him to become a

Catholic? And you could never have gone along with his idea of becoming a Trappist!"

"You're being very free with your conclusions, Goodheart. What do you know of what I may or may not have gone along with?"

"Oh, sir!" But then I was speechless.

"As the French say, *Pour les grands maux les grands remèdes.* Nick was a deeply troubled soul. He needed the kind of support that the Roman Church offers to some of its converts. And I think he even needed the bulwark of the Trappist discipline. There are different ways of coming to God. I believe he may have chosen the right one. For him, anyway. I pray for him. Do likewise, Percy."

I hardly knew that morning in my sacred studies class what I was saying to my students in our discussion of Saint Luke as the author not only of his gospel but of the Acts. My head was aswirl over the revelation that one of our foremost priests had actually recommended to a man his conversion to Rome and his submission to the Trappists! It would have defied my imagination had I not been prepared for a new insight into the insidious danger of evil. If Satan was working in the soul of the bewitched headmaster, was not God working in mine?

I had always in mind a talk I had, one Sunday morning after chapel, when Mr. Lyman Rice, visiting the school for a meeting of the trustees, had taken me firmly by the elbow and guided me into the garth for a brief stroll and a confidential chat.

"I know, Goodheart, that your duties take you closer to the headmaster than any other teacher at the school, which is why I am saying what I have to say to you. You are in a unique position to observe Dr. Lockwood in the performance of his multiple duties. The board is aware, of course, of his advanced age, and although we fully appreciate his continued fine physical strength and mental capacity, we wish to know if he shows any sign of strain or weakness. We are in a position to come to his assistance with any aid that he needs, like expert medical attention, extra stenographic or administrative help, even a limousine and driver, anything to lighten his load. He, I know, would never ask for these things, so I'm going to count on you to give me the word."

On Mr. Rice's next visit, I requested a private interview, and he took me for another walk in the garth. I shall never forget how his features turned to stone when I told him what Lockwood had advised his son.

———

When it was announced that the headmaster would retire at the end of the current school year, no reason was given, nor was one necessary, as his departure date coincided with his eightieth birthday, which was a time for even the greatest head to step down. There were rumors that Mrs. Lockwood had intervened to persuade him to give up his post, and I could well imagine that Mr. Rice had perhaps not even consulted his board, but had simply, in personal converse with the great lady, whose influence on her husband, if rarely exercised, was still paramount, convinced her that a silent withdrawal would eliminate the furor that might well be aroused by any public airing of the facts.

The whole world, it seemed, now burst into plaudits of the great man's long distinguished career and accomplishments. The campus was inundated with alumni coming to bid farewell to the revered pedagogue; newspapers and editorials trumpeted his prominence in the field of private education. He was too occupied now to see me nearly as often as he had, and on the few occasions that we still met, he gave no indication that he had the least suspicion of what I had done.

But, oh, that brings me to the heart of the matter and to the cause of my crackup. He said only one word to me, but that word was enough to shatter my entire nervous system. On Prize Day, after his moving farewell address to the boys, the faculty, and the crowd of visiting parents and alumni, the masters of the school lined up to grasp his hand in a final tribute. I, as the youngest member, came last.

Taking my hand, he smiled and pulled me close to him and whispered in my ear that one word before turning away. *Judas.*

3

THE CALL OF THE WILD

I HAVE NEVER HAD a friend quite like Harry Phelps. Everyone has always liked Harry, well enough, that is, but there was a general feeling that he was something of a bore, however harmless and amiable a one. He had an even temper—remarkably so, you never saw him either depressed or elated—and a bland, round countenance, a strong stocky figure, a thick head of black hair, and large, rather expressionless blue-gray eyes. Some women credited him with a subdued sex appeal, but his nature was certainly not a passionate one. Nor did he ever say anything particularly witty or even very interesting. Yet you could count on him. He was there, so to speak, always reassuringly sympathetic. He was like a glass of milk, and you couldn't be drinking Scotch forever, could you? He was certainly a loyal friend.

Nor could he be pushed around too much. He could be directed, yes, he could even be bossed, as we have seen him be, shrilly, by Lola, his first wife, but there were still things about which he could be immovable: his Saturday game of golf, his summer fishing trip with old college pals, his pipe and favorite radio program, his early morning calisthenics. Lola would break her fingernails in any effort to interrupt these. He was like a domestic animal that would submit meekly to be trained in certain routines but could be adamant in rejecting others.

And the animal is not a bad analogy, either, as Harry, like one of them, saw no difference between himself and other members of his species. Animals are not snobs, and Harry appeared to make no distinction, say, between the fashionable society of his parents' world and the sundry employees of his brokerage firm on Wall Street. He treated everyone in his same mild and modest way. People who met him had no notion of a social register background or an elite private schooling; these things had washed off him without leaving a trace.

I remember at the New England boarding school in which we were classmates, at age fourteen, before our voices had changed, that we were both cast as sopranos in the chorus of young maidens in a performance of *The Pirates of Penzance*. While delivering one of our songs, Harry noticed that his shoe had become untied. Calmly, stolidly, he leaned down slowly and carefully to retie the laces, utterly indifferent to or at least unconscious of the fact that he was breaking the orderly line of the singers. After the performance the outraged director was heard to exclaim, "Harry Phelps has no idea there's anyone in the world but himself, and he never will!"

Life, however, doesn't depend on one's performance in amateur theatricals, and Harry passed easily enough through school and college and took his place ultimately in his father's small brokerage house. He was the only child of very stylish parents who had just enough money to maintain their constant round of visits to the homes of their very much richer friends. The Gerald Phelpses were a handsome, beautifully attired, highly ordered, and disciplined couple of exquisite manners who played excellent bridge and golf. They were utterly baffled by Harry, but saw that he did well enough on his own and left him, after a few vain efforts to make him more socially presentable, pretty much to himself. This was fine by him. The only unfortunate part of their detachment was in their failure to prevent his picking Lola as his bride, or rather his being picked by Lola as her husband. Not that Mr. and Mrs. Phelps approved of Lola; they simply threw up their hands when confronted with her aggressive personality, her olive complexion, and sharp black eyes. She came from a dull, respectable family on the edge of the Phelpses' fashionable world, close enough to be recognized and snubbed by it. But Lola knew enough to bypass them and go directly after Harry. He might not have been much, but she was shrewd enough to see that he was the best she could get.

In my observance there are two kinds of nasty women: those who can be agreeable when they get what they want, and those who remain disagreeable even afterward. Lola was of the latter sort. She was one of those tormented souls who is always unhappy and wants everyone around her to be as unhappy as she is. Harry bowed meekly to all her demands: how the children should be educated, where the family should spend their vacations, what friends they should see, on what objects their money should be spent, even what church they should attend, everything, in short, except in the few areas of his pleasure specified earlier. Of course, these were just the ones she had to go after. Her possessiveness was satisfied only by totality; any reservation outraged her. But Harry was a rock when it came to these few retentions, and their domestic life was rent with turmoil. The two children, a docile son and a daughter who was her mother's clone, had been drafted into the maternal alliance.

I can see now that there may have been a latent cruelty in Harry's submission to Lola in so many aspects of their existence. Her tantrums brought her no relief; she would have been happier without them. Had Harry only once said to her quietly, "Lola, I am moving out of the house. When you have calmed down and decided to be reasonable, I shall consider returning," and acted on it, I have little doubt that she would have collapsed. And been the better for it. She needed a firm hand to steady her in her near fits. But it was never stretched out to her.

I did not find Harry and Lola's home a pleasant place to visit, and through the years I saw him mostly at bimonthly lunches at our downtown club. My law firm represented his brokerage house, and we occasionally had some business to discuss, but for the most part we simply exchanged items about old school and college mates. And so passed a decade and a half.

The abrupt change in our talks came about one day when he brought me a startling piece of business. He announced it, however, in his customary dry tone, and for a moment I was too stunned to reply. He wanted me to represent him in a suit for divorce that Lola was bringing against him.

When I spoke I was still too amazed to be tactful. "What did you do that finally broke the camel's back?"

"I rejected her plea for a reconciliation."

"Then you aren't going to oppose her?"

"Not in the divorce, no. But her terms are confiscatory."

"I suppose she wants the kids. That's natural. You can always get visitation on holidays and summer."

"It's not that. She can have the children. It's my money I have to look out for."

"Well, of course you'll have to give her a chunk of that. A big chunk, too. That's inevitable."

"You don't get it, Peter. She wants everything I've got. Right down to my last cuff link. I'm perfectly willing to be reasonable, even generous. But she wants to see me begging on the street corner with a steel cup in my hand."

I stared. "Harry, what have you done to her?"

"It's not so much what I've done. Though that's certainly in it. It's what I plan to do. I plan to wed Marianne Sykes. Do you know who she is?"

Well, I did know. My firm represented *Athena*, a well-known liberal literary quarterly, with a reputation for controversy, that was backed by a wealthy woman client of ours. Marianne Sykes was one of its principal editors, and I had used her as a witness in defending the magazine against a libel case. And a very competent witness she had proved. She was a handsome, self-assured woman, with a reputation for being hard-boiled and famed for her biting wit. She was somewhere in her thirties, considerably Harry's junior, and I knew she had been divorced at least twice. What in God's name was a woman like that doing with Harry?

"And she wants to marry *you?*" I couldn't help it. My tact was gone.

"I know it's odd. She thinks so herself. But she fancies me. She likes me in bed."

"Harry! Is this really you talking?"

Instead of returning to our offices after lunch, I took him down to the club bar where we drank an unprecedented postprandial liqueur, and I got the whole story out of him. This is what he told me.

"You know that as counsel to *Athena*, Peter, you were kind enough to recommend my services to any of their editors who needed investment counsel. That is how Marianne

Sykes came to me. She had a modest sum to place in the market, and I had the luck to make a good little profit for her. She was pleased and invited me to one of her magazine's cocktail parties. It was July, and Lola and the children were in Maine, so I went alone. Of course, I didn't know any of the literary celebrities who were there, but I enjoyed watching them. And then, to my surprise, when I was leaving, she hooked her arm under mine and said, 'How about buying me dinner? Didn't you say you were a summer bachelor?' Well, of course I was delighted to take such a brilliant woman out, and we went to a neighboring restaurant and drank a good deal of wine while she told me some awful stories about the people we'd just left. She can be wickedly funny, you know. After dinner I walked her home to her apartment, and she asked me up for a nightcap. And do you know what, Peter? I didn't even hesitate. I went right up!"

"And then it happened?"

He nodded several times. "Then it happened, indeed. After our first drink, she suddenly stood up before me and started to unhook her blouse. She simply asked, 'Well, are we going to fuck or aren't we?'

"Peter, I was stunned. As you know, I never use four-letter words. My time in the navy sickened me of them. It seems to me that they turn the world into a brown stink. But I have to admit that the word she used was just the right one for what we did that night. She stripped off all her clothes, as easily as if we'd been a married couple, and told me she had no use for foreplay. And her body, Peter! Her flesh was firm, her skin like ivory. I guess I went kind of crazy. It wasn't simply the most wonderful thing that has ever happened to me. It was the *only* thing that has ever happened to me!"

"And for her?"

"Oh, for her, naturally, it was something much less." Here he actually shrugged. "I'm not a total fool, Peter. I know she has what the auto dealers call mileage. It's not only that she has had two husbands. There have been plenty of other men, too. She makes no bones about that. But she liked what she did with me. Oh, yes, I could tell that. And she's willing to repeat it."

"How did Lola find out?"

"I told her. I had to tell her when I said I wanted a divorce."

"My god, Harry, was that necessary? A one-night stand when your wife's away and you've reached a dangerous age is no reason to wreck a marriage. Even Lola might overlook it."

"Indeed, Lola offered not to overlook it, but not to let it break up our marriage. After her first terrible fit, she was ready to keep me if I promised never to see Marianne again. But I have every intention of seeing Marianne again. I have every intention of marrying her."

"Does she insist on that?" I could hardly believe that she did.

"Not insist, no. But she's willing to give it a whirl if I obtain my freedom."

"Harry, can't you see that marriage means nothing to a woman like that? Sure, she fancies you now, as she says. You've given her some kind of a new jag, despoiling the innocent, perhaps—I'm sorry, but I must be frank with you—and when she's through with you, she'll toss you away like a bit of used Kleenex. And what will you be? A plucked chicken!"

"I know the risks, Peter. And I'm willing to take them.

Certainly, there's something in what you say. But look at the other side. She's younger than me by six or seven years, yes, but she's still on the wrong side of thirty. Probably closer to the fatal forty than she admits. Brilliant and attractive as she is, husbands don't exactly grow on trees at her age, and she's too smart not to know it. I may not be such a bad investment, after all. The magazine world is notoriously fickle, and she has small means. And at the worst, marriage will give me more time with her. I'll be harder to shed."

"Not much harder."

"But some."

"Harry, you're a damn fool!"

"Do you think I don't know that?"

Of course I agreed to take the poor guy's case. But there was little I could do to reduce Lola's voracious demands. When she had at last recognized that there was no chance of preserving her marriage, she had turned on Harry with an appalling hate, backed by a bloodhound of a lawyer. I could barely wrench a pittance of visitation of the children out of her claim for total custody, and my efforts to see that Harry retained enough of his property to live decently were constantly undermined by his anxiety to get the wrangling over with and wed his inamorata. In the end he yielded Lola full title to their house with all its furnishings, sixty percent of his income, and a goodly slice of his capital. What can you do when a client collapses on you?

I was also dismayed by the fierce unanimity with which his old world turned against him. His parents, his family, his friends, even his business partners swelled the chorus of popular outrage at his conduct. I could hardly believe that I was living in an age where divorce had become almost as accepted as marriage. What had aroused these hot denunciations of adultery and home-wrecking? What had Harry done to bring back the ghosts of Queen Victoria and John Calvin? The only way I could make any sense out of it was in the theory that what people find hardest to forgive is any fundamental change that a man makes in what they have deemed the final classification of his character. Is it not a hint that their critical faculty may not have been as true as they have believed? That a libertine continues to be a libertine is acceptable; what is troublesome is when he turns into a saint. Likewise, a dull, disciplined husband who has been certified as utterly harmless and dependable must not evolve into a rake. Harry was unforgivable and unforgiven.

I did my best for him, but my case was undermined by his eagerness to obtain a rapid release from his matrimonial bond. And when he married Marianne—for she did agree in the end to have him—he rejected my urging him to tie her down with a premarital agreement and executed a new will leaving her everything that Lola had not grabbed.

I will admit that Marianne was not mercenary. She had total confidence as a provider for herself and never gave a thought to any future financial emergency. Money was of little importance to her, and she spent freely and carelessly any that came into her hands. Harry bought her many things that she not only didn't need, but didn't even much want. What was worse for him, however, was the considerable sums that she took from him to loan to talented but deadbeat literary friends. And when she accepted an offer to teach English for a year at a famed western university without even consulting Harry, he took a year off from his work to accompany her. Coming back he found his percentage of the firm's profits drastically cut, and he resigned in a huff. He was reduced now to living on the remnant of his capital, facing actual poverty when that should be exhausted.

Of course, Marianne left him. That had always been in the cards. But she left him not because of his decreased means, but because she had met her fourth husband at the western university, and she shed poor Harry just as she would have shed the piece of used Kleenex that I had once likened him to. She never even raised her voice. Harry was simply as if he had never been. She didn't ask for a penny of alimony and paid her own lawyer in the speedy divorce proceeding.

When we lunched, he and I, after the decree came down, at what was now my but no longer his club, to discuss what the future might have in store for one so stripped of everything, he still insisted that what he had done had been worth it. The one thing he still seemed to care about was making me see this.

"Marianne gave me the only life I've ever had," he kept saying.

"Oh, Harry!" I cried at last in an exasperation I could no longer suppress. "Do you really call *that* life? And all of life, too?"

"I can try."

I refused to discuss it further. I simply couldn't. He had shocked me to the core of my being, and I didn't really much care what happened to him now.

THE CONVERSION
OF FRED COATES

LORNA COATES was a very proud and bitter woman. She was herself of an army family, and she had fallen in love with her handsome and stalwart husband when he was an aide to her father, a brigadier general stationed in the Philippines. She had envisioned a career that would ultimately take him to a president's staff in Washington, and, if he had the good luck to serve in a war, to the high national awards of heroism. And indeed the brave year 1917 had brought the desired Armageddon, and Stanley Coates, to the trenches in northern France, but a tragic tactical error on the part of his commanding officer, which was to some degree unfairly attributed to him, resulted in long postwar assignments to obscure army bases. Her husband, Lorna indignantly believed, could have saved his reputation with a candid revelation of just what had happened at the battlefront, but with stubborn rectitude and misguided loyalty he had insisted on sharing the blame with a superior who was only *too* willing to dilute his own guilt. Though devoted to his wife, Coates was deaf to her pleas in what he deemed a case of personal honor, and he accepted the lifetime consequences of his silence with grim but uncomplaining reserve. He had the total courage that sometimes accompanies a total lack of imagination.

Lorna had now only her son, Frederick, as her one hope

for the larger life. She was determined that he should not follow his father in a military career; she saw, clearly enough, that in America the path to glory was nearer to Wall Street than to West Point. She taught the boy never to be distracted from a goal by an idle enthusiasm, or, particularly, by an idle animosity. "The world is largely run by fools," she would warn. "They must be suffered not gladly but mutely. Let them have their silly gods, their inane causes, their cherished fetishes. Never make an enemy until you're sure his teeth have been drawn. Even religious maniacs should be tolerated. Their god, note, is hungry for praise. Even an eternity of anthems won't satisfy him. Why do they worship him? Because they believe he has power. Which shows they at least have the sense to know that power is the supreme thing. Very well. Let us have power. I don't mean riches or thrones or having people bow down to you. That's just vulgar. I mean power to sway the destinies of man. For man's greater good, of course. And for your own good, my boy."

When Fred was fifteen and attending high school in San Diego, where his father was then stationed, his mother determined that he should go to Chelton, a prestigious boys' boarding school in Massachusetts that had recently established a scholarship for the sons of military officers. She applied successfully for this without telling her husband. Coates at first objected to sending his son to an academy where he would be associated with boys so much richer, but he encountered a resolution in his wife so furious that he soon abandoned the fray, consoling himself with the notion that the Great Depression, through which the country was then passing, might reduce some of the Chelton parents to an economic level not too distant from his own.

Fred had already developed into a sober, thoughtful, closely observant if somewhat detached youth. Fortunately for his mother's plans for him, he was remarkably handsome. His wavy auburn hair, strong regular features, serious gray eyes, and fine muscular figure, always so darkly and neatly clad, attracted the admiration of both sexes. But perhaps his most winning quality was the grave attention that he accorded to those who conversed with him. He was a good listener, and his short comments were to the point. His grades were the highest in his class, and his skill at games, if less notable, was adequate, but his inclination to isolate himself, without betraying any contempt for the crowd, somewhat dampened the popularity that he initially evoked.

Fred respected his father without missing any of his limitations, and he thoroughly understood his mother and the dreams in which she indulged about his own future, while carefully weighing their extravagance. He harbored an ambition quite as great as hers, but, unlike her, he knew the dangers of letting it be seen. The lesson that he had best learned from her was that a man's truest friend, perhaps his only real one, was himself.

———

At Chelton he found he was in a new world, but not one for which he was unprepared. The sons of eastern bankers and corporate lawyers, who deemed him at first a somewhat alien body, soon came to respect his easy proficiency in class, his agility on the field, his quiet manner, and his ready fists if antagonized. As the students were not allowed to have any cash on their person but small change for Saturday afternoon purchases at the local village drugstore, there was no way for the richer ones to display their family's wealth but in more expensive suits, which meant nothing to other boys, or boasting, which only brought them jeers. There was no racial or religious discrimination, as there were no Jews or blacks or Latinos, and very few Catholics or foreigners (a tiny group of diplomats' sons among the latter), and Fred's classmates enjoyed a social equality among themselves, for which he was gratified that he did not have to struggle as his mother had taught him to expect. He even discovered that his army background had an exotic flavor to a few of his new friends. It was true that his parents never came to visit the school in a Lincoln town car or a Hispano-Suiza as some other parents did, but then, finding travel across America a needless expense, they didn't come at all. Fred came to Chelton without attachments, and attachments could be liabilities as well as assets.

Chelton was an Episcopalian Church school, and religion was heavily emphasized by the veteran cleric headmaster who, hale and hearty in his seventies, had been principal when half the students' fathers had been his pupils, and who was regarded as a kind of deity by both the boys and their families. But Fred soon gleaned that the Reverend Doctor Emerson could be easily handled: all he really required was that the boys should *look* respectful and God-fearing when in chapel or when any topic of faith or morals was discussed. Outside of these all freedom of thought and much of action was permissible, but freedom of thought by no means implied freedom of speech. The first rule of a Christian society was a rigid prohibition of any articulated criticism of its accepted mores. Grant that, and you could do pretty much as you liked. It was not difficult. For example, Fred observed that almost none of the Chelton graduates went into either politics or the ministry, despite the thunderous urgings of their revered and totally sincere headmaster, but instead dedicated their lives to commerce. Yet this seeming inconsistency was rarely mentioned. Chelton, to the families that supported it, was a virtuous and noble institution essentially divorced from the real world, but an excellent training ground for youths who would thereafter wear its high standards like a brilliant feather in their hat. It was essentially a decoration, yet it had a distinct worldly value. It meant something to be a Cheltonian. And Fred was going to be one.

How did Chelton deal with sex? Doctor Emerson's principles at least were made very clear. Absolutely no sexual activity, solitary or in couples, could be tolerated outside of marriage. Yet the reverend headmaster demonstrated an uncomfortable and wrathful awareness that despite all his preaching and the threat of immediate expulsion from the campus, there were boys addicted to unseemly experimentation in this area, and prone to something he denounced from the pulpit as "sentimentality." It was notorious among the students that the old man must have learned about this in his own boyhood at a public school in England, where his father had been an ambassador. Fred was quickly aware that these "experiments" were being carried on by a goodly number of his classmates after lights-out in their dormitory, and they did not seem oppressed by the least sense of sin. It was again the double standard.

He himself was not intrigued by mutual masturbation or sodomy. He developed an interest in girls earlier than other boys, and there were no girls at Chelton or even a pretty woman among the chambermaids and waitresses selected by a housekeeper trained by the vigilant headmaster. His good looks, however, invited a fair number of lewd propositions from some of his classmates. These he declined, but always in such a way as not to appear offensively prudish. "Sorry, pal," he might mutter. "I guess I'm too much of a damn Christer." Sex, no doubt, would have its role to play in his career, but not yet. In the meantime, what did it matter what others did or didn't do? He had taken to heart his mother's warning about making unnecessary enemies.

Sex did, however, have one indirect influence upon him. Alistair Simpson, the golden-haired, blue-eyed, but somewhat effeminate and delicate son of Chelton's richest alumnus, was attracted to Fred by something considerably stronger than the smutty physical curiosity of rutting boys. Yet Alistair, despite inclinations of which he had not yet gauged anything like the full force, was a prude who was shocked by the nocturnal activities in his dormitory and clung as tightly as he could to Fred, whom he extolled as his virtuous hero. He insisted that the latter visit him at his home on a spring vacation when it was too far and too expensive for Fred to travel to his own. It was in the great red-brick Georgian mansion of the Simpsons, on a thousand-acre plot in Westbury, Long Island, that Alistair's new best friend first met his formidable father.

Edgar Simpson, the Wall Street banker, was as large and hearty and stentorian as his high position in the world of finance seemed to require. He had four daughters, all attractive and self-possessed, all older than Alistair, but the latter, as an only son, received his father's particular attention and caused his particular disappointment. Edgar loved the boy in his own possessive way, but he wanted to make much more of him than was obviously possible, and he chafed openly at his frustration. Fred, who visited Westbury again in the summer, possessed, as the banker soon perceived, all the qualities that were missing in his son, and he wondered if some of them might not be transmitted to his heir by a kind of osmosis. When the boys were in their last year in Chelton and the choice of a college became an issue, Mr. Simpson, on a visit to the school, invited Fred, without Alistair, to lunch with him in the local village inn. This was most unusual for a visiting parent to do, but nobody questioned Mr. Simpson, who had given Chelton its new gymnasium and hockey rink and might even do more.

Fred was thrilled by his ride to the inn in the backseat of the rattling, shining Isotto Franchini that was sent to pick him up. It was the way he traveled in his dreams. At the destination, he was ushered into a private dining room where Mr. Simpson offered him a rum cocktail against every school regulation. Fred knew he was perfectly safe in discreetly sipping it. His host went straight to the point.

"I'll put all my cards on the table, Fred. I'll start by admitting that I've had you and your background thoroughly checked out. I know what a fine soldier your father is and that he has not been promoted as he should have been. I know that he is a man of honor and that he has paid debts incurred by his own father, which he was under no legal obligation to do, and that this has left him financially straitened."

Fred simply nodded. It was not for him to criticize what, from a less powerful man, might have been deemed an unwarranted invasion of privacy.

"I know too that you have been an admirable son and have never exceeded what, at least by Chelton standards, must have seemed a slender allowance. And you have been a fine friend to my son, helping him in his studies and protecting him, as he is not strong, from bullying boys at school."

"He's been just as good a friend to me, sir, as I to him," Fred replied stoutly. "Maybe it's a case of what in biology class we call symbiosis."

This was not true, as Fred was well aware and, as he suspected, Mr. Simpson was equally aware. But it sounded good, which was what counted, both to the latter and to himself. Fred had written to his mother about his friendship with Alistair and his visits to the Long Island estate, and she had encouraged him to cultivate so advantageous a relationship. "You'll be doing as much a favor for that boy's father," she had written, "as he can ever do for you. I miss my guess if a keen tycoon like Mr. Simpson won't hang on to someone who can bolster the weakling I gather his boy is. Perhaps he sees you as the son he really wanted. It's only kind to comfort a disappointed parent." Fred's mother had a quality rare in ambitious mothers: she perceived the value of perceived kindness in one's ascent in the world.

Mr. Simpson nodded, a bit perfunctorily, to acknowledge Fred's overstatement of his debt to Alistair. "It's nice of you to say that, my boy. And it gives me further assurance of the value of your friendship with him. Certainly, it's only natural for a father to be more concerned with what such a companionship does for his son than what it does for you. But I wish to benefit you as well as him. Alistair is going to Yale. I want you to go with him, and I want you to room with him there. But I understand that this might be a heavy strain on your father's budget. I should be happy to supply your tuition."

This was not altogether a surprise to Fred, as Alistair had already hinted at the possibility. He knew of his father's hope that he would undertake a military career, but he was also aware that he could count on his mother to stifle any such hope. One of her firmest resolutions—and these were very firm—was that her son should not be trapped in what she called the cul-de-sac of the army. Fred was certainly going to take Mr. Simpson up on his generous offer, but first it was in the interests of his dignity to convert a gift into something more like a contract.

"Father is very keen on my going to West Point," he observed, "and he may be in a position to get me a preference there. There would be no tuition, and I have had to give the matter a good deal of thought. But I must admit I've had some doubts about an army career, and the prospect of Yale with Alistair is certainly tempting."

"Well, think it over anyway," Mr. Simpson said, in a tone that seemed assured of a favorable answer. Had he fathomed Fred's purpose in his seeming stall? And if he had, didn't he approve? Weren't they basically, Fred wondered, two of a kind?

Of course, he didn't have to think it over. He and his mother had already prepared his father for the likelihood of his matriculation at Yale. And his final year at Chelton was something of a triumph. He was elected one of the seven prefects who helped the faculty in the administration of the school, he was editor in chief of the *Cheltonian*, president of the debating society, and his diploma was engraved with the Latin phrase *summa cum laude*.

Yet he had a somewhat disturbing chat one morning after a class in English with Mr. Baxter, the wise old head of that department and known as the most intellectual master at the school. Baxter had asked him to remain after dismissing the others on the pretext of discussing Fred's paper on Trollope's *The Way We Live Now*.

"You know, Fred," he began in an informal and friendly tone, "that I often feel we put too much stress on extracurricular activities in a boy's last year at Chelton. The graduating class has to run so many things: the school paper, the dramatics, the debates, the crew, the football team, and so on, so they have no time to . . . well, to find their souls. And isn't it a time to do so? They are really already men."

"I don't quite see what you mean, sir," Fred replied a bit uneasily, for he tended to shy away from the abstract.

"I wonder if you don't. I've had an eye on you, my lad. A friendly eye, I should add. Take this paper of yours—for which, incidentally, I'm giving you an A. Aren't you perhaps implying that Trollope is pulling his punches?"

"How do you mean, sir?"

"That he doesn't really believe in the happy ending of his novel. In the collapse of the villain Melmotte's fraudulent money schemes and the triumph of the good guys. That Trollope has supplied all that for his rosy-eyed Victorian readers though he knows perfectly well that the monkey business of London's financial world is going to go right on as before."

"And you're suggesting that it wouldn't? Is that your point, sir?"

"No, I'm not concerned with Trollope's London. At the moment I'm concerned with a bright young Chelton sixth former called Frederick Coates. Does he regard his about-to-be alma mater as a dim bulb lit by those who vainly hope it will illuminate a dark world? A world that nothing can illuminate? And is the said Coates one of the rare few who sees the hopelessness?"

"And if I did see that," Fred said, after a considerable pause, "how do you suggest it would affect me?"

"Wouldn't the temptation be to live entirely for yourself?"

Fred stared, with a sudden, almost eerie fascination, into the sad but kind eyes of this intently gazing old man. Was the door of a new communication actually opening a crack for him? It was interesting; it was on the edge of being exciting; it was somehow dangerous. Not only for him, but perhaps also for Mr. Baxter. He parted his lips to answer, but then closed them. Didn't he see something else in those searching eyes? Couldn't he make out that the dim bulb was what Mr. Baxter himself dreaded to see as the image of the school to which he had given his all? And if that were the case, what would the poor fellow's life amount to?

"No, sir," he replied firmly. "I don't see Chelton that way at all."

"Well, perhaps that's just as well," said Mr. Baxter with a sigh.

———

At Yale, Fred and Alistair, though roommates, began to go their different ways. The friendship remained, but Alistair was growing restless under the other's semi-tutorial role. He was still his amiable, easygoing self, and he still attracted the few classmates he took the trouble to meet, but he went to New York every weekend to satisfy a professed passion for the theater. He drank more, and Fred suspected that his once latent but now emerging homosexuality accounted for his absences as well as for his taste for Broadway. Ultimately, in his sophomore year, after a thunderous row with his father, he dropped out of Yale altogether and took up abode in Greenwich Village, living comfortably on the ample income that his death tax–saving parent bitterly regretted having settled on him. The latter's affection for Fred, however, survived his rift with his son. He recognized that Fred had done everything for Alistair that could be done, and he continued his financial support, even to some extent putting his son's friend into the filial space in his heart that the son had abandoned.

Fred was quick to note that at Yale Chelton was not quite the ticket to campus success that he had hoped, for his classmates from there tended to be cliquey and to associate with their counterparts from St. Mark's or St. Paul's, while the graduates of larger preparatory schools, like Andover and Exeter, dominated the social scene. Fred easily affiliated himself with a group of men whom he spotted as campus leaders: they ran the *Daily News*, the Political Union, the more exclusive fraternities, and became members in their final year of one or another of the six secret societies. The group, closely knit, had distinct common denominators: they all came from more or less privileged Protestant Anglo-Saxon families; they all had been privately educated, and they all were endowed with a highly patriotic and idealistic desire to become responsible and liberal leaders in law or business or even politics. The Roaring Twenties were out of fashion, the cloud of the Great Depression had lifted, and the rise of dictators in Europe gave the boys the needed foe to raise a glorious standard against. Most of them opposed their fathers in their enthusiasm for FDR and his New Deal.

Fred saw in them the wave of the future. There was nothing in their creed that he could not easily and convincingly adopt. But unlike them there were things he observed that they didn't. He noted that, although, with apparent sincerity, they roundly condemned any form of discrimination, there were no Catholics, Jews, homosexuals, indigents, or radicals among them. He likened the group to what in early Victorian days Disraeli had called Young England—graceful, youthful aristocrats of mildly liberal views. These observations, however, he did not feel obliged to share with his new friends.

Yet he did make one friend outside of this group, Nathan Levy. Nathan was the son of a prominent New York newspaper owner and a member of a prominent German-Jewish family. He had a long, dark, handsome oval face and thick, sleek black hair; he was supposedly intensely intellectual and was an editor of the *Yale Literary Magazine*, but he held himself somewhat aloofly from the undergraduate body, as if he considered himself above boyish amusements. He was also reputed to embrace leftist political views and to be on the outs with his influential parent.

Fred, as an editor of the *News*, first got to know Nathan when he induced him to review for the paper a play, which, as many dramas then did, was opening in New Haven before assailing Broadway. It was a parlor comedy satirizing the apoplectic opposition of Wall Street to the New Deal, and Nathan's review had been brilliantly witty but also scathing. Fred, who had assumed that Nathan would have approved of the play, asked him what had caused his harshness.

"The play is full of sham liberalism" was Levy's relaxed, rather drawling reply. "The kind of crap the more intelligent conservatives put out to make the masses feel that Tories are basically liberal. Sometimes they almost mean it. But it's still crap."

"But if they almost mean it, maybe they're almost sincere."

"Who cares? It's easy to make fun of extreme right-wingers. They're so absurdly pompous. But people like the author of this silly play fundamentally dote on the very things they purport to satirize. Like Marquand and O'Hara, for example. They pine for all the shiny baubles they jeer at: the swank clubs, the exclusive parties, the smart set, the whole world of money and privilege. Like Thackeray and the lords and ladies he professed to mock. Or Proust and the duchesses whose asses he kissed."

Fred was amused. "What writers are there who are genuine liberals?"

"There are plenty, but unhappily they're apt to be unreadable."

"So the Tories have it all to themselves?"

"You should know, Coates. Didn't you go to Chelton?"

"That I did. But it seems to me that you go rather too far. Look at my friends here on the *News*. They all believe in a better world. In a less hierarchical society. In a fairer distribution of the wealth."

"Oh, yes, I know those preppies," Levy retorted sneeringly. "I went to Ames Academy myself. Not exactly Chelton, to be sure, but along those lines. I know about their ideals. I know they want to be as pure as King Arthur's knights. But at heart they're full of the old school spirit. Over or under but never around! Our team must never lose! Wave the stars and stripes above their heads and they'll fight for the devil himself. Oh, yes, they're brave enough. But they can be had. Courage is cheap. Physical courage, anyway."

"I wonder if I don't need to see more of you," Fred said thoughtfully.

"Any time, fella. Be my guest. You have an army background, don't you?"

"You seem to know everything."

"Oh, I keep my eyes open. You may be a brand to be plucked from the burning. The army *and* Chelton! Wouldn't that be a feather in my cap!"

This conversation took place in the fall of Fred's junior year, and in the months that followed he saw Nathan Levy frequently and read some of the socialist and Marxist literature that his new friend provided. He found the relationship stimulating; a philosophy that annihilated the individual in view of the general well-being intrigued him. It seemed to offer a relaxation from tension at the same time that it provided a goal for action. Didn't it basically make life easier? At least simpler?

He didn't have to introduce Nathan to any of his old group, as Nathan had no interest in them, and as they, for all their stout denial, would have shown little enthusiasm for a Jewish radical. Faced with these two supposedly liberal doctrines of his Yale experience, Fred felt he had to choose between the one that regarded FDR as the leader who had saved the nation from revolution and the one that had branded the president as the force that was holding back the uprising that would redeem the world.

The choice became critical that spring when Fred was told by friends that he was likely to be tapped, as it was put, for membership in the senior society Scroll & Key. This select group of fifteen seniors, who met twice a week in a windowless stone building where they presumably discussed their souls and futures, was not quite so prodigious as Skull & Bones, which claimed the leaders of the class, but it was distinctly more "social" and was rumored to be the *Open, Sesame* to many a paneled door on New York's Wall and Boston's State Street.

"This is the ultimate test, Frederick Coates," Nathan warned him solemnly. "As a Keys man you'll be forever lost to us and wedded to the establishment."

Fred did something he had never done before: he turned to another for advice. That other was Mr. Simpson, his guardian angel. But Mr. Simpson was a Keys man from Yale, 1905. And Fred knew that! Didn't that mean, he asked himself feverishly, that he had already made up his own mind? Well, what if he had? Hadn't Simpson paid his bills? Didn't that create at least a moral debt? Or were there no moral debts, except to oneself? Well, there he was!

He supposed that Mr. Simpson would be thoroughly disgusted with him for even raising the question and that the great banker would berate him for picking a left-wing Jew as an acquaintance, let alone a friend. He might even threaten to discontinue his financial support. But mightn't that be the ultimate test of Frederick Coates as a man? And didn't a man have to meet it squarely? There were times when he reminded himself that he was, after all, the son of a brave army officer.

What he faced, however, when he went down to Mr. Simpson's great Wall Street office, was a very different kind of test.

"I'm glad you came to me, my boy. A bright young man like yourself is bound to have doubts sooner or later about the way his world is run. He is something of a dope if he doesn't. And that is the time when the bad men who are dedicated to overthrowing our republican form of government get to you. It so happens that I know this Nathan Levy's father. He is a fine man and an excellent newspaper editor. We are not friends, for I do not happen to choose my friends from Jewish circles. But I respect him, and he respects me. We have cooperated on some financial reports. And he confided in me once, when we were discussing the youth at a lunch, that his son was flirting with communism. He was deeply upset."

Fred's discussion with Alistair's father lasted for an hour. When he took his leave, he asked for news about his former roommate. Mr. Simpson looked very grave.

"Fred, I am appalled to say that Alistair is in the deepest kind of trouble. He was arrested last week for soliciting a boy in a public urinal. My lawyers are trying to get the wretched business quashed. No, don't say anything. Don't even try to see him. I have him out on bail in the country. Go now, please, my boy, and remember what I've told you."

He gripped Fred's shoulder, but then turned abruptly away and returned to his office, leaving his young friend to take his dismayed and thoughtful departure.

Some weeks later, on Tap Day, Fred stood in Branford Courtyard with others of the Yale junior class, as members of the senior societies circled among them looking for their nominees. At last he felt an impact on his shoulder like Mr. Simpson's final touch, and heard a voice behind him bellow, "Go to your room!"

And he went.

———

Fred entered Yale Law School, still supported by his Wall Street backer, and with him went many of the earnest and ambitious members of his prep school crowd. Nathan Levy had made up with his own father, at least enough to be given a job on the latter's paper, and he disappeared from Fred's life. There had not been much left of their friendship in their final year; Nathan had assumed that Fred's inclusion in a senior society had cooled his interest in a person so removed from campus enthusiasms. Fred worked industriously as a law student and was elected an editor of the *Law Journal*, which virtually assured him upon graduation of being employed by any of the great Wall Street firms that he chose.

He knew that Mr. Simpson was ready to offer him a fine job and a rosy future in his bank, but he was keen on practicing law, and he decided, correctly as it proved, that the latter would accept his choice so long as he agreed to become an associate in the firm that represented the Simpson interests. As this firm, Shepard & Bates, was one of the most prestigious, Fred, his mother, and his angel were all content. Alistair Simpson, who had been somehow extricated from his jam, had been sent abroad indefinitely, and Fred was more than ever in his place.

Fred had now put together precisely the kind of career for which he meant to devote his mind, energy, and heart. He had never quite forgotten the concept of a life devoted to a cause as opposed to personal success, and he had combined it with the more worldly but still sufficiently noble image of the great public servant espoused by his other Yale group. The career of the senior partner of a notable corporate law firm who, now possessed of ample riches, took his proper place in national affairs as an ambassador or a cabinet officer, seemed to offer just this—an Elihu Root, a William Maxwell Evarts, a John W. Davis. Such a man would not have to soil his hands, in Disraeli's horrid phrase, by shimmying up "the greasy pole" of elective politics; he would be appointed by a president and approved by an admiring senate.

There was first, of course, for Fred and for his generation, a war to be won. He chose the navy as the cleaner and more picturesque service, became an ensign, and served creditably on an aircraft carrier in the Pacific, where he had the luck to be mildly wounded in an air attack on his vessel and awarded the Purple Heart. He had dissuaded Mr. Simpson from using his influence to obtain a safe shore job for him in the navy department where, as the latter coaxingly put it, his "expertise in the law would be more useful to the war effort." He had sensed that a combat record would account for more kudos when peace returned. That he might be killed was a matter of indifference to him. Once a career had been decided on, one had to pursue it regardless of risk. If one was to be a great man, one would probably survive. Napoleon, in all his battles, was wounded only once, and Theodore Roosevelt escaped a rain of bullets on San Juan Hill.

After the peace of 1945, Fred's career swept forward as if on wings. He rapidly became an expert in securities law and the right-hand man of the senior partner, Phineas Bates, who was the very prototype of the great man he sought to become: a big, bluff, cheerful, dominating figure with tousled gray locks and cool gray eyes. He was a wily and imaginative attorney, a compelling orator, and the father of three bright, chirping, idealistic daughters who worshipped him and among whom the handsome Fred wondered if he could not find the mate he needed. Naturally, he would have to become a partner, but this rank was accorded him at the early age of twenty-nine.

He spent many weekends as a guest of the Bateses in Westchester County, for his boss liked to work on Saturdays and even on some Sundays away from the city, but he was careful to see that the tasks of his assistant were varied with strenuous tennis matches and dinner parties attended by his lively wife and daughters.

Anita was the oldest of the latter and perhaps her father's favorite. She was not outstandingly pretty, and her figure, if compact and well-shaped, was a bit on the sturdy side, but there was an exuberance in her manner and a candor in her laughing blue eyes that charmed all but the sourest misogynist. Anita loved the world and wanted it to love her. But she was far from dumb and even able to be shrewdly critical; she might give you more credit than you deserved for living up to her own high moral standards, but if you fell too obviously below them, she could manifest a sharp and articulate indignation.

Fred had never questioned the tradition that a good wife was a vital element in any successful American career, and he had every intention of finding one for himself. He might be cool, certainly, but not cold, in his way of going about it. His consort would not have to be rich, as he expected to be an adequate provider, but neither should she come from impoverished or lower-class parents. It was incumbent that her background and upbringing not be a cause of awkwardness in any social circle to which they might aspire. It was also desirable that she be in love with him, or at least enthusiastically cooperative in sexual matters. He was not such a fool as to underestimate the havoc that a discontented spouse might reap in a man's life. She must be made happy, or at least contented, and he supposed with some reason that he could count on his own nature to be a faithful and considerate husband. Was it so difficult? And were not his standards common to many sensible and intelligent men, however little expressed?

Anita came to know him as well as any girl had on the

weekends when he was her father's working guest, and from the beginning he enjoyed the advantage of having the latter's total approval. Indeed, he was almost thrown at her, which is not always the best way of improving a relationship. But his good looks and seemingly modest yet self-assured good manners, his easy competence on the tennis court and in the swimming pool, his flattering interest in her accounts of her job at *Vogue* began to stir a deeper feeling in her heart. And when she at last perceived that she had won his friendship without capturing anything stronger from him, that he might even be a man whose passion she might never be able to arouse, she of course fell in love with him.

Even when he started to take her out, on nights when he was not working late, he did not change his ways. He talked always interestingly about his job, his future hopes, asked about her life and friends and plans, even discussed current events and the darkening cloud the cold war was casting over Europe. But he rarely spoke of his family, his boyhood; he seemed to exist only in the present. He never made a pass at her, and he never even sought a good night kiss when he took her home to the family brownstone. He did not even seem to suspect that she might have liked it.

And of course she loved him more and more.

And then, one night, dining at a restaurant, he asked her to marry him. Just like that. As if he were suggesting that they go to the theater rather than to the cinema. And she accepted him. Just like that. He signaled to the waiter and asked him to bring them a bottle of champagne. When it came, and their glasses were filled, she found the courage to ask, "Do you know something, Fred? I have this crazy idea that you're acting a part."

He took this calmly enough. "In a play? What sort of a play? I hope at least that I'm the hero."

"Oh, you're the hero all right. But it's not so much a performance as a rehearsal. There seems to be a director sitting out there in the orchestra. In a front row seat. But it's dark, and I can't see him. Oh, I know it sounds silly, but you're going to have to get used to my being silly at times."

He frowned, and she observed that it was a new kind of frown, or at least one that she had not noted before. "And what does the director do?"

"Well, he's ready to supply you with a line. That is, if you forget one."

"What line have I forgot?"

"Well, you haven't even told me that you love me."

He became grave at this. "I love you, Anita."

And she believed him. She had to believe him. But she also had to add something. "I love you too, Fred. Very much. Very, very much. But maybe I'm just a tiny bit afraid of you."

He shook his head as if she had raised a more important issue than she knew. "If you're afraid of me, my dear, you had better not marry me."

"Oh, I'm not *that* afraid of you!" she cried in sudden excitement. "Don't think you can get out of this that easily!"

The first year of marriage was, on the whole, eminently satisfactory to both husband and wife. Fred continued to be the same pleasant and even-tempered companion that he had been as a beau, with the all-important added attraction of being an ardent lover at night. One of Anita's pals assured her that this was often true of young lawyers who had been monastically devoted to their work too long. Anyway, it came as something of a surprise to her and helped smother the little misgivings that she had felt about what she was almost hesitant to call his occasional detachment. She even joked to herself about being an Elsa in *Lohengrin*, too wise and too happy to ask her lover's name and see him sail away in a swan-propelled boat.

———

A few years into their union, Anita's father had been appointed an assistant secretary of state by President Eisenhower, and he had asked his son-in-law to head up the important branch of their firm in the capital. Bates might have been motivated in part by the desire to have his daughter near him, but Fred saw it as a promotion that would bring him closer to the post of heir to the senior partner that he coveted. So all was well, or so it seemed. He and Anita had a charming little house in Georgetown, and she was expecting their third child.

One day, passing through a corridor of the State Department, where he had been calling on his father-in-law, Fred encountered his old friend Nathan Levy. The latter informed him that he was now a special assistant to the secretary of commerce, and suggested that they have lunch. Fred, interested in catching up with this once stimulating acquaintance, took him to the Cosmos Club, which he had recently joined, and quizzed him about the apparent switch in political views that his current job implied. But Nathan seemed more anxious to quiz his host.

"You've really made it, Fred, haven't you? But then there was never much question that you would."

"How do you mean?"

"You always set yourself in a beeline for the top spot—that was clear enough. And what's wrong with that? So long as you get there, and you have, my friend. In your job, in your marriage, in your future. I'm not criticizing you. I think I may even envy you."

"What about yourself?" Fred queried with more than a touch of resentment. "Haven't you done pretty well, too? You don't look to me like someone who's sharing the crust of the poor."

"No, I live well enough. But that's dough I inherited."

"And your job in Commerce. Isn't that something?"

"It might have been." Nathan's tone changed from his old ironic note; he suddenly seemed human. It was evident that he wanted a more candid discussion. "But you know, Fred, we're living in a reign of terror. At least those of us in government are."

"You mean this McCarthy business. That's odious, of course, but isn't it bound to go away? It's so obviously a red herring, and the guy's such a phony. Won't it be a case of not being able to fool all of the people all of the time?"

"Maybe. But will there be anything left when it's over?"

"Surely you're exaggerating, Nate."

"Am I? Who's going to stop McCarthy? Will Ike? Will Dulles? Will your esteemed father-in-law? Have any of them lifted a finger to defend loyal government employees maliciously accused of treason? And whom they know, or should know, to be innocent?"

"Ike may be playing for time. Give the junior senator from Wisconsin enough rope and he'll hang himself."

"Dream on, pal. And in the meantime our sainted president won't even defend General Marshall, to whom he owes his entire career, from McCarthy's spit."

"I admit that bothered me," Fred conceded.

"I tell you, my friend, we tore up the Constitution when we put thousands of Japanese Americans in concentration camps without trial, even though they were innocent American citizens. We left the field wide open for little Joe to ravage as he chose!"

"That was wartime fever. Crazy things happen in war. We all know that. Anyway, you have nothing to fear from the Un-American Activities Committee personally, I assume. So why get quite so upset?"

"Oh, but I have! I have! I have every good reason to believe that I am on Senator Joe's list of government suspects."

"In the Commerce Department? Why in God's name does he care what goes on there? What could he charge you with?"

"With giving classified information to an agent of the Soviet Union. Isn't that the usual charge?"

"But you didn't!"

"Of course I didn't. Does that make any difference? You'll say they can't prove anything. But anything is just what they can prove to a hysterical jury. I tell you, a man accused is a man doomed!"

For the rest of their meal they discussed the fabrications of the McCarthy committee, and Fred found himself both intensely interested and strangely wrought up. He told Nathan that he would like to renew their aborted Yale friendship and invited him, still a bachelor, to the house for dinner. Nathan came readily enough, and made an immediate friend of the enthusiastic Anita.

"How absurd," she told her husband afterward, "to suppose that he could be suspected of being in the pay of the Russians. Isn't he the son of a rich man?"

"And he's also one himself. Yes, he was something of a radical at Yale, but that's a far cry from being a communist, let alone a traitor."

"What could he have in Commerce that the Reds would really want?"

"Oh, I don't know. Trade agreements, I guess. Or the confidential talks preceding them. Or department plans to root out communists in government. And I suppose that an idealistic American communist might not have to be paid to betray his country. He might even be wealthy and guilt ridden. But I'll stake my last dollar on Nate's loyalty."

"Oh, darling, so will I! And I can't tell you how much I love hearing you say it!"

He looked at her in mild surprise. "Why do you love that so much?"

"Oh, just because I do!"

In the weeks that followed, Fred saw Nathan at several lunches and had him over for dinner a couple of times as well. It came, therefore, as less of a surprise when Nathan called to say that he was about to be indicted. Fred went at once to his apartment—Nathan had already resigned from Commerce—where he found McCarthy's victim astonishingly calm, almost indifferent. Fred assumed that receiving the blow might have been an actual relief from the agony of anticipating it. But when he informed Nathan that he wished to act as his counsel, the latter was suddenly touched and rose to grasp his friend's shoulder.

"Look, old man, that's going too far. Not that I don't appreciate it, I do, deeply. But when I tell you that the lawyer in the attorney general's office who will be in charge of my prosecution is none other than Hallam Daly, on leave of absence from your own firm, you will see the impossibility of it."

"I also can take a leave of absence!"

"And anyway, I have my father's firm to represent me."

"I could be co-counsel, couldn't I?"

Nathan appeared suddenly struck by the idea. He pondered it for a moment. "It would be rather a jab in the prosecution's eye," he admitted. "But what might it do to your career, my friend?"

"I don't care! Some things have got to be beyond that."

"Well, we'll sleep on it."

Fred's visit to his father-in-law at State, where he went immediately after his visit to Nathan, was stormy. Bates was appalled by his son-in-law's proposition.

"But I know he's innocent," Fred protested.

"How can you *know* a thing like that?"

"Think how long I've known him. And haven't I heard you yourself say that most of McCarthy's victims are blameless?"

"I never said they all are. I know nothing about Levy. Neither does Mr. Dulles. The matter has nothing to do with State, and I certainly don't expect to get into it. You will do very well to follow my example."

"I'm afraid I can't go along with you there, sir."

"You can't? What's got into you, Fred? I've never seen you worked up like this before. All about some Jewish radical you haven't seen since college. How do you know what he may have been up to since then?"

"I have my conviction that he's not guilty."

"Very well, let him prove it. And as for your representing him, you must see it's out of the question. You know who's in charge of the prosecution. How can you appear against your own partner?"

"I can take a leave of absence, as he has. Neither of us will then be active members of the firm."

"You'll still be partners. The canons of ethics won't allow it."

"Then I'll resign from the firm altogether."

"You can't do this, Fred!" Bates exclaimed with sharp dismay. "You can't do it to your wife and children. You can't do it to me. You can't do it to yourself!"

Even in the painful distress of the scene unrolling before him, Fred found an odd little part of his senses that seemed to be telling him that he was becoming someone he had never been before—a curious distortion of Frederick Coates, conceivably even a not very appealing character. But one who was going to stick. In the back of his mind, he could hear that old hymn they used to sing at Chelton: "Once to ev-er-y man and na-ation, comes the mo-oment to de-cide." Was he going crazy?

"I think I know, sir, what I have to do" was what he heard himself say.

"Fred, listen to me. If you won't think of yourself and your family, think at least of your political party. It's the party that has taken me into government and will take you in time, if you'll just keep your head. We have an election coming up, and there's every reason to hope for a Republican sweep. It's no time to show a rift in the ranks. Ike will take care of McCarthy in time—don't you worry. But right now we have to do a little ducking before this storm of spy catchers. Granted, a few people will get hurt who perhaps shouldn't get hurt, but that sometimes has to be accepted. First things first."

"I guess that depends on what you regard as first things."

This was not, of course, the last talk Fred had with his father-in-law on the subject. Bates even brought two of his older law partners down from New York to argue with their stubborn junior. But Fred was unyielding. The biggest surprise in the whole affair for him was Anita's explosive support of his stand. He had rather assumed that she would change her tune when it came to opposing her adored father, but on the contrary, the parental confrontation seemed to add to her fire.

"Be the man I married," she urged him at one point, when the force of the partnership began to look as if it might be too much for him, "and not the man I almost didn't."

When he finally sent in his formal resignation to the firm his mother wrote him a long bitter letter berating him for tearing down everything she had spent her life building up. And Mr. Simpson wrote to say that he felt he had wasted his money and sympathy supporting a man who was now willing to jettison the accomplishment of a lifetime to come to the aid of a Jewish communist.

———

As it turned out, however, it was not Senator McCarthy who had instigated the prosecution of Nathan Levy. McCarthy's committee had sniffed around the Department of Commerce, but it was the FBI that had set the attorney general on Nathan's trail. At the trial Fred's services were indeed used by Nathan's father's lawyers, and he was allowed to cross-examine one or two hostile witnesses, but the major part of the proceedings was in the hands of his co-counsel, and he spent many hours sitting silently beside his friend and offering him such tacit support as he was able. But the testimony of a double agent that revealed Nathan had indeed passed classified information to a Soviet agent relating to commercial treaties between the United States and Israel resulted in Nathan's conviction.

Fred, reeling at the catastrophe, sought an interview with his client alone. He stuttered something about the probability of a reversal on appeal.

"Not in this day of hysteria," Nathan replied in a surprisingly mild tone. In fact, he seemed to accept his doom as something nobody should waste time trying to avert. "I've had it, and I face it. It was always in the cards that this might happen. I knew the risks, and I took them of my own volition."

"What the devil are you trying to tell me?"

"Didn't you ever suspect it, Fred? I thought you probably had, but that you believed fighting McCarthy was right on any grounds."

"Oh, my god, Nate, how could you have done a thing like that? How *could* you? Betray your country!"

"Because the Soviet Union is the only nation in the world that genuinely desires peace. I hoped that the info I gave them might prove some help to their putting pressure on both Israel and Palestine to work things out. I failed, and I'm through. But others will take my place. No, Fred, don't try to argue with me. You could never be brought to see the light on these things. You are too committed to the old rotten order of the world. It's not your fault. It's the way you were raised."

"Nate, is it possible that with all the evidence of the atrocity of Stalin's murders, you still—"

"Spare your sermons, Fred," Nathan interrupted firmly. "They're wasted on me. I'm not saying that I approve of everything that goes on in Moscow, but I adhere to the longer, the larger view."

Fred walked home from the courthouse, block after traversed block, his eyes on the pavement before him, grimly facing the bleak fact that his life was in tatters. He had lost his firm and his reputation. Any political future for him with the Republican Party was gone for good. He had alienated his mother, his father-in-law, his early sponsor, and for what? To defend a confessed traitor.

Anita listened to his sad tale and then disappeared without a word. He heard her steps descending to the cellar. When she returned she was holding a bottle of champagne.

"We'll have to put ice in our glasses," she told him. "Do you want to get some from the pantry?"

"What in God's name are we going to celebrate, I'd like to know?"

"Our grand new life!"

"Darling, have you taken leave of your senses? Have you heard what I've been telling you?"

"Of course I heard you. But don't you see? You've spent your life doing the right thing for the wrong reason. Now, at last, you've done the wrong thing for the right reason. You are *you* now, my dear one. And you're never going to be anyone else as long as I can help it!"

He stared at her in astonishment and at last smiled. He went to get the ice.

THE OMELETTE AND
THE EGG

KATE RAND had imbued her philosophy of life—that of a
dedicated domestic wife and mother—from her own mother.
Emma Laidlaw, a highly intelligent, smartly efficient, brisk
but kindly lady, tall, straight, and strong, both in character
and figure, had been left in 1900 a widow of limited means
with six children at the age of forty. The Laidlaws were a huge,
gregarious Manhattan tribe, some rich, some almost poor.
Emma was nearer to the latter. Her assets had been a small
portfolio of securities, an ordinary side street brownstone
and three housemaids, a cook, a chambermaid, and a nurse,
little enough in the opulent east side of the city of that day,
where Irish servants were paid a pittance. But it was gener-
ally agreed among Emma's more affluent friends and rela-
tions that her skill in management amounted to genius. She
was an expert cook and housecleaner when the servants had
their rare days off; she was as good as a trained nurse when
the children were sick; she drove a car before other women
did and was clever at picking up stock market tips from the
magnates she sat by at dinner parties. She knew just how
to get her well-mannered children invited by richer friends
or cousins with children the same age to go on trips or stay
at country resorts, and even made those friends think she
was doing them a favor. She became such an asset to host-

esses, as much by her keen suggestions about how to make a party go as by her ability to charm and regulate bores, that she was able to carve out a permanent niche for herself in the top echelons of Knickerbocker society, assuring her offspring of the help of the powerful in making their way in life.

Kate, her eldest daughter and most faithful disciple, saw little better to do than to copy her remarkable parent in every way she could. She was aware of handicaps in herself totally lacking in her mother: she was more timid and shyer and in-clined to give a romantic imagination too much leeway, but she had willpower, and Emma was a tolerant and benignant teacher. Nor did she ever try to persuade Kate that men were in any way either to be blamed for exerting dominance over women or deserving of such dominance. In fact, Kate sus-pected that her mother thought that few men had the ca-pacity to accomplish what she had accomplished. Whatever force had created men had made them what they were, and that had to be accepted. And, anyway, in ceding them the world of downtown, were women ceding them anything that women really wanted?

Both Kate and her mother were avid readers, and the spare moments of a busy day were apt to be devoted to books, particularly to fiction. Kate's favorite hour was the one before supper, which Emma, even on nights when she was dining out in the great world, reserved for reading aloud to her older children. Kate, as the eldest, sat in an armchair, while two of her sisters cuddled by their mother on the sofa, and, resting her head back, eyes closed, she absorbed the clear tones that unfolded the adventures of David Balfour or David Copper-field or Henry Esmond. Could she ever dream of composing such tales herself? Impossible thought! Yet her mind was full of plots.

When she matriculated at Barnard College in 1910, she spent much of her freshman year composing a novel about a spoiled debutante who flees the dull and conventional husband her snooty family has picked for her with a seemingly romantic lover who turns out to be duller and much more malevolent than the spouse she has abandoned. The ending was too preachy, as her mother gently pointed out, when Kate gave it to her to read.

"But your tale has its moments, my dear," she added. "It's far from contemptible."

Far from contemptible! Her *Madame Bovary!* "You think I could never be a real writer!" Kate cried in bitter disappointment.

"Never, as they say, is a long word. I think you may always be able to contribute pieces to be read and enjoyed by your friends. And you might well become a first-class letter writer, an art that is sadly neglected today. But never forget, dear girl, that the world we live in has need of all kinds of doctors and lawyers and businessmen, both first-class and second, and maybe even third, but it has no need of any but the first-class in writers and artists."

"And you think I'd be a third-class writer!"

"Darling, I can't tell at this point. Do you want me to say I see another Edith Wharton in you?"

"No. But you don't seem to want me to be a writer at all."

"I don't think it's the happiest life for a woman, no. If you look at the famous woman authors, you'll find them a rather barren lot. Mrs. Wharton has no children. Neither did Jane

Austen or George Eliot or Sappho—so far as we know—or the Brontës—"

"Charlotte was pregnant when she died!" Kate interrupted.

"But she died, didn't she?" At least Emma smiled when she said this.

"And Elizabeth Barrett Browning had a son!"

"Who turned out badly. But let's not get too serious about this. Writing is a dangerous thing because everyone thinks he can do it, and lives can be wasted in the effort. Write what you want, but don't get stuck in it. Remember that life is just opening up for you. Don't let it pass you by!"

Kate's spirits were dashed for a time, but she recovered them. Her mother, after all, was her idea of a great woman, and it should not be altogether impossible for a daughter to become something not too unlike her.

Emma and her widespread Laidlaw connections had their worldly side, but they kept it in reasonable check. A studious girl like Kate should certainly have been given full rein to take advantage of her courses at Barnard and spend some of her evenings scribbling, but the social side of life was not to be ignored, and she had to submit to a small dinner dance given her by one of Mama's well-endowed cousins and to attend a certain minimum of balls. After all, a girl was not likely to find a husband in the Barnard library.

Kate submitted to all this with a good enough grace, and even enjoyed some part of it. Her looks were only modestly pretty, but she danced well—Emma had seen to that—and she talked less idly than some of her contemporaries, who thought young men liked that, which, alas, some did. But she had one row with her mother. She had been taken into a sorority at Barnard, and her initiation had fallen on a day she had accepted a dinner invitation. Her mother refused to let her out of it, and, reluctantly attending it, Kate had met her future husband, Howard Rand.

Emma always maintained afterward that this proved the value of putting first things first. "In our society," she firmly declared, "when you accept an invitation to dinner, you go or send your coffin."

He was a modest, appealing, attractively shy (at least in female company), and good-looking youth who came from a family that was in every way, except socially, the opposite of the Laidlaws. The Rands were dull, stuffy, and ultra-religious; they had brought over from the Scotland of their remote origin as much Calvinism as their little storm-tossed vessel could carry. Poor Howard fell below their standards as effectively as Kate before those of the Laidlaws, though in a very different fashion. His total lack of interest in church or Bible, his early habit of hanging out with boys of ungodly thoughts and doings, his frank distaste for the dark orderly life of his clan had caused him to be actually disliked by the prudish little valetudinarian, self-obsessed mother who ruled the home and received the gawking worship of his silly, temperamental sisters. His initial self-confidence had been undermined more than he knew by the loveless disapproval of his widowed mother, and he found himself much at a loss in the mirthful company of the more sophisticated Laidlaw crowd. It was to the quiet Kate that he turned.

"It must be great to live in a family where everyone enjoys themselves," he confided in her once. "My sisters go to parties, but they have to be home by midnight on Saturdays, and that's just when the real fun starts."

"You mean they mustn't dance on the Sabbath?"

"Or do anything else but look gloomy and pray."

"What about you?" They were eating supper in a free corner of the Plaza ballroom at a debutante party, and it was ten minutes after twelve.

"Oh, me too, but I stay up. Mother has threatened to lock me out, but she's afraid I'll get into worse trouble. Though I don't know why she cares, as she thinks I'm bound to hell in any case. But what can she do? I'm over twenty-one."

"She could cut off your allowance."

"I have a small trust that Dad left me. It's not much, but I could eat. It would get me through law school, anyway. I've only another year to go."

"So you're going to be a lawyer."

"If I can land a job."

"Is that such a problem?"

"Not if Uncle Jules Anthon kicks in. He's Mother's brother. Has a big firm downtown."

"Why do you need him?"

"Because my grades aren't much. And they weren't at Yale, either. I have to admit it, Kate. I'm no shining light. Mother says I wrecked my chances at college by coming down to New York every weekend to see girls."

"And did you?"

"No! I came down to see one girl. Julia Shelburne. Did you ever know her?" He suddenly seemed eager to be confidential, obviously unaware of the tactlessness of holding forth on a girl other than the one he was with. But she found that she didn't mind it. She didn't mind it at all.

"Julia Shelburne," she repeated, bringing to mind a tall plain girl of supposed wealth. "Didn't I read that she was engaged to some prince or other?"

"You did," he responded sourly. "Some slimy, mediatized German semiroyalty who's after her chips."

"Why do you assume that he's mercenary?"

"Oh, they all are. Everyone knows that. But I didn't give a hoot about her money! I even hated it! In my dreams she had lost it all! I used to tell her that if we ever married, we'd give it all away. Oh, I was crazy. Can you believe it?"

She nodded. "I can." And she did.

"She didn't seem to mind. She liked me. I know she did. We used to write each other long letters. And then her father took her off to Europe where he was an ambassador, and I wrote her that she'd meet all kinds of dukes and earls and never think of Howard Rand again. And do you know what? She never did!"

Kate was so surprised that she laughed. It was the right note, however, for after a moment he laughed too, and then added sheepishly, "I shouldn't be boring a pretty girl with my silly problems."

"You don't bore me, Howard."

"Well, you're not like your cousin Millicent Laidlaw then. *She* gets bored quickly enough."

"Yes, when the subject changes from Millicent Laidlaw being the belle of the ball. I'm glad you don't find me like her."

"You don't care about being the belle of the ball?"

"Not in the least."

He glanced at the dance floor, where some couples had returned from their supper tables. It was certainly a pretty sight. "You're an unusual member of your family, Kate. But I like that."

"Oh, I'm the black sheep! I frown on them. Yet all those dear cousins, they're harmless enough, really. They want only to have a good time. It's my fault that I can't help seeing them as having something in common with all those amiable French aristocrats who gambled and gossiped and made love in the revolutionary prisons while awaiting their turn at the guillotine."

"Kate, what an image! Do you think we're in for a reign of terror?"

"Well, maybe not quite that, but life always has some sort of comeuppance. The Laidlaws have guts, I admit. They would greet disaster with a shrug and a quip. Style to them is everything. But to me life needs something more than style."

"Such as?"

"I'm not sure yet. But I know I'm going to take things more seriously and more literally than my family does."

"Maybe you'll be a lawyer or doctor. Many girls want to try that these days."

"And I applaud them. But I don't think they ought to marry. I still think a mother's first duty is to her children. Marriage in the old sense seems to be going out of fashion, and I wonder if it's not a great mistake."

"What do you mean by marriage in the old sense?"

"Something that every member of the family it produced treasured and tried to preserve. A bond that held parents and children together in love and mutual respect. Fathers who didn't spend their weekends on the golf course but devoted the bulk of their spare time to being with their sons and daughters. Mothers who weren't always playing cards or dining out. Children need a mother at home, despite what the modernists say."

"It doesn't sound much like my family," he said with a

wistful shrug. "When I was a boy we hardly ever saw Dad except when he took us to church. And Mother was always resting. I can't remember a time when our nurse, with a finger on her lips, wasn't warning us that Mother was resting."

"Was she ill?"

"She certainly thought she was. But I guess it was more that she found the world too noisy for her nerves. She surely found me too noisy. I think her attitude toward men—of whom I'm afraid she saw me as the worst example—was that they owed it to women to be constantly apologizing for their crudeness."

Kate reflected on this. "I wonder if you ever had what I call a real family."

She was soon to meet his mother, for in the following weeks Howard became a steady beau, and Emma Laidlaw was vocally enthusiastic (to Kate, rather humiliatingly so) about her having caught an admirer. Even caustic old Grandma Laidlaw, though she hankered for in-laws far richer than the Rands, was heard to concede that catching Howard Rand might be better than being the last leaf on the tree. To her, who had been wed at seventeen, Kate at twenty was already an old maid.

Her first dinner at the Rands was a family affair. Mrs. Rand, a small, tight-lipped lady, with unwelcoming pale eyes, presided stiffly over a table where her three daughters sat mostly silent, except for their half-smothered giggles over something whispered to one another, which elicited the maternal stare of disapproval. Mrs. Rand asked Kate some perfunctory questions about the Laidlaws that seemed to indicate that the speaker's acquaintance with them was not likely to be further cultivated. The black paneled walls, the heavy Victorian silver, and the portraits of grim, humorless forebears made for a depressing interior. Kate suspected that her hostess may have regarded Howard's bringing a girl into their midst as an invasion of her privacy by a difficult and untrainable son. The difference in Mrs. Rand's tone when she addressed her son was in marked contrast to the one she used for her daughters. They might be silly sheep but they were *her* silly sheep. They hadn't gotten away from her. Yet. Howard had. Or had he?

"Mother's not quite as bad as she seems," he suggested rather desperately afterward to her.

"Isn't she? I wonder if she's not worse." For already she had begun to see that someone needed to take this young man in hand, and she wondered if it might not be she.

At home with her own mother, she reflected on how utterly different the latter was from Mrs. Rand.

"Did Mrs. Rand say anything about your family?" Emma asked Kate. "I suppose she thinks we're a pagan lot who dance and drink and should all be burned alive in Times Square in some Presbyterian auto-da-fé."

"No, I think she'd let us off with a whipping."

"I'm glad you don't feel you have to stand up for your boyfriend's family. You've kept your head, child. Good. I suppose the Rands have held on to some of that old shipping fortune, though they say Howard's father was dumb as dirt and that you could sell him the Brooklyn Bridge. And his wife goes on as if she wasn't the only person left to remember what her family used to be. That's always a sign that people are poorer than you think."

"Howard will make his own way, Ma."

"We can hope so, anyway."

"The Rands seem to live well enough."

"In a brownstone, like everyone else, except a few Astors and Vanderbilts. You can't tell until you see how they live in summer. But if you and Howard ever make a match of it, you'll have to free him from his family. I daresay it can be done."

Kate had to admit that her mother had a point. Howard had not received at home anything like the approbation that so amiable a youth should have expected. Everything natural about him as a boy—his high spirits, his pranks, his slang that he picked up from his school friends, his yanking the hair of his shrieking sisters, his muddy shoes on the carpet—had genuinely repelled his orderly and bitterly conventional mother. The poor boy had been made to feel a disgusting creature for the very features that might have endeared him to another parent. A father might have adjusted all this, but his was dead.

At last Kate came to recognize that this seemingly independent and strikingly attractive young man, whom even her Laidlaw cousins didn't disdain, was actually turning to her for some apparently needed support in his daily life. When he was not with her, he was even writing to her.

"A talk with you works wonders in clearing my mind," one letter confessed. "After a hard week of torts and contracts and corporate reorganizations, my head is spinning, and I begin to doubt if I'll ever make a lawyer. But then you tell me about your courses at Barnard and all the books you've been reading and the people you've seen and all the funny things about them you've so wittily noticed, and then everything comes back into focus for me. You're so sensible, Kate, so sane and measured, and I'm so mixed up about what I want and where I'm going. I really need you to be my friend."

A crisis now arose that drastically altered Kate's relationship with her admirer. For three weeks there was a sudden silence between them—he neither wrote nor called. She was concerned; indeed, she was surprised at how much she was. But she didn't feel that their friendship had reached a point where she could reproach him for this. She knew her mother to be the last word on such matters as how far a girl could go without appearing too bold or pushy, and she was driven to consult her.

Emma listened with a mild but definite interest. It was quite clear to Kate that her mother deemed Howard no great catch but perhaps as good as her daughter would do. It might be just as well to hang on to him.

"Why not write him a short note, simply saying you hope he hasn't caught this nasty spring cold that's going around. When I go calling this afternoon in Aunt Amy's car that she's lent me for the day, I can drop it at the Rands'."

"You don't think it would look too forward? It isn't as if we were engaged or anything."

Her mother laughed. "Well, I hardly thought you'd have engaged yourself without telling me. And as for 'anything,' I've no doubt you're a virtuous young lady. But I'm sure there's no harm in showing him a bit of friendly concern. We can carry artificial manners too far, you know. That's how your cousin Millie lost that Morgan boy."

"Well then, I guess I'll write him."

"And don't use the best notepaper. I feel that letter is going to be drafted several times."

In the end the letter was never sent, for a totally unexpected thing occurred. Howard's mother called on Kate.

"I know you may think this odd of me, Miss Laidlaw, but

my daughters have persuaded me that you're the only person who might be able to bring Howard to his senses. I'm sorry to have to tell you that he's been acting most peculiarly. He's saying he won't go back to law school or take his exams, and he spends his days roaming sullenly around Central Park. And I'm afraid I detected liquor on his breath. Would you talk to him, Miss Laidlaw? I should be grateful."

Kate knew that only a very serious crisis would have brought a woman as stiff as Mrs. Rand to this appeal. It was agreed between them that Howard be told that she would meet him outside the boathouse in the park at noon the next day. And of course he was there ahead of time, waiting for her, his face drawn and haggard.

They strolled together for an hour while she did most of the talking. She had learned from her new friends at Barnard that depression could be a real disorder and not just what the Laidlaws called "dumps," something to be cured by a sharp bid to "pull up your socks." A better instinct impelled her to tell him, at the cost of any old-fashioned maidenliness, how much she needed him and how little she minded his giving up the law so long as he didn't give up their friendship.

And as his face lightened she began to realize that she had won. He would give up neither.

He graduated respectably in the middle of his class at Columbia Law School, and Uncle Jules Anthon proved good on his promise to take him on as a clerk in his Wall Street firm. His salary, plus his modest trust and Kate's allowance from Grandma Laidlaw, enabled them to marry and maintain a small but comfortable apartment until better pay and infants should come.

Kate was never entirely sure whether she had fallen in love

with her charming but vulnerable spouse or with her mission to save him. Did it matter? He was always in love with her, and they were soon enjoying the family life she had so long extolled.

2.

In a later time Kate would be given to imagine that her lifetime would be limited to three score years. The extra biblical ten might be eliminated or given her in some form of senile incapacity—she didn't care. But the sixty her mind would divide into thirds: her youth, her marriage, and her discovery of herself.

The second score had been happy enough, certainly as happy as she had ever expected it to be. She and Howard had had little money at first, but they had made out, and when the magnificent Uncle Jules Anthon, he of the haughty stare and drooping moustache and upward tilted chin as depicted in the austere portrait in the Downtown Association, died suddenly of a stroke, Howard had been swept in as a partner in the reconstruction and large expansion of the old firm by its new chief, the renowned New York ex-governor Clarence Cook, who had been convinced that Anthon's nephew was a part of his legacy. Howard at any rate had worked out his own specialty in the new and grander firm: he headed a small real estate department, largely a personal service for clients and partners who had residential purchases or sales to make, and hardly a big moneymaker in a great corporate law factory. Still, it was useful for the partners not to have to go to outside counsel—often potential client stealers—for deeds and mortgages, and Howard did his work with painstaking care. Besides, he was greatly liked in the firm, which he tenderly regarded as his club or fraternity as well as his office.

Kate was busy enough with her household, her five children, her settlement house, her book class, and her occasional small dinners for clients and friends. Above all, she had the satisfaction of a contented and devoted husband who asked for nothing better in his free time than to be with her and their offspring and who showed no signs of a return of the nervous malady that had almost wrecked his law school career.

But there were moments—how could there not have been?—when she caught herself wondering, Is this all there is to life? To *my* life anyway? And then she would sternly remind herself how much more sensible and decent and even civilized was the world in which she now lived than the one where so many only played and laughed. The lawyers and clients in Howard's firm were good and serious citizens conscientiously engaged in keeping the wheels of finance and business on which the nation depended smoothly turning. They were mostly good family men, too. And the members of the great banking establishment that was the principal client were revered in Wall Street like the twelve apostles!

Yes, of course women—and God bless them—were invading fields long monopolized by men, but that did not have to mean that those who occupied themselves with home affairs were wasting their lives. The great majority of the consorts of Howard's partners and clients were still housewives like herself.

Yet one incident, seemingly trivial and totally unrelated to these speculations, aroused an unexpected anxiety when she found it persistently returning to mind. During a summer vacation in the Hamptons, the Rands had accepted an invitation to a large dinner party to be given by Mrs. Lars Samson, an imposing elderly widow, described in society columns as "the reigning dowager of the dunes." On the morning of the party, the sun arose on a day of halcyon weather, a cloudless blue sky and an even bluer sea. The young tutor Kate had hired to help her keep the children amused and happy informed her that he had organized a beach picnic that night for the children and their friends, and Kate was suddenly appalled at the prospect of missing it. To have to give it up on such a day for a stuffy dinner of old bores? Surely Mrs. Samson, a fundamentally nice woman with children and grandchildren of her own, would understand if she gave out and told her honestly why. Had she consulted her mother, her mother would have warned her — her mother, alas, was dead. She gave out on her hostess.

But all she got when she did so on the telephone was the great lady's crisp "I see. I shan't expect you then."

Two weeks later, when she encountered her disappointed hostess at the Beach Club and ventured to tell her how sorry she had been to have to miss what she was sure had been a wonderful party, Mrs. Samson had said simply, before walking on, "I had been going to ask you and your husband to another gathering when my daughter comes to visit, but then I thought, no, you'll be doing something with the children."

That night at dinner Kate realized that she could not tell her husband about this incident. It might have upset him, as Mrs. Samson was a client of the firm. Not that he would imagine that she could be so petty as to change counsel over so small a matter, but still . . . What really bothered Kate was her sense of the image of herself in the old lady's mind. It must have been of a fussy, nervous, pea-brained mother who couldn't leave her progeny even when she had a staff to help her. Was it for this that she had so restricted her life?

She had no friend with whom she cared to discuss so deep and intimate a question, but she had one whose company she more often sought now that such a question had arisen to trouble her. Rosina Hudson was a person who differed widely in her tastes and preferences from other women in the world in which she and Kate both lived. She was old New York; indeed, none were older—she descended from the hardy captain of the *Half Moon*—but she was not only unmarried, she was perversely content not to be. Yet she was certainly not one to affect masculine airs: she arrayed her slender torso in floating silks that went well with her long dark hair, her high pale brow, and the thickly rouged lips from which she emitted her languid drawl. Miss Hudson was much smiled at in Kate's world, but everyone knew her—had always known her—and a grudging tribute was paid to the fine taste that marked her jewel of a duplex in town and the perfect little Palladian villa in East Hampton that was a veritable museum of old master drawings and bronzes. Rosina was not as wealthy as her grander neighbors, but she had a sharp eye that could single out the one peerless print in the art gallery, and her long tapering index finger was the first to point out the priceless porcelain in the back of the crowded cabinet.

What Rosina lived for was beauty, which may have explained why she was so much more discriminating in her selection of objets d'art than in her selection of friends. She was perfectly willing to confine herself to the restricted society in which she had been raised, and had no objection to philistines at her small, elegant dinner parties or in her box at the symphony so long as they were sober, punctual, and appropriately clad. Perhaps she even enjoyed feeling superior to them. But when, as with Kate, she spied something in the nature of a similar intellectual bent, she could even exhibit excitement. When Kate was elected to the ladies' literary reading group, of which Rosina had long been the unchallenged but hard to follow leader, and had eagerly seconded Rosina's unpopular motion to devote three meetings to the great trio of Henry James's late style, the two had almost embraced.

Nor had it taken Rosina long to discover that her new friend was hoarding critical talents that should be cultivated at whatever cost to the domestic routine in which she seemed so deeply enmeshed. Might it not be the duty of the descendant of a great discoverer to discover a talent long smothered in the clutter of homely tasks? But Rosina was no fool. She saw that she would have to go slowly with one as committed as Kate to the supposedly here and now.

Arguing that they needed deeper and fuller discussions of literature than those provided by their fellow members of the book class, who were mainly concerned with which characters in a novel they "liked" or "disliked," Rosina persuaded Kate to a weekly lunch of just the two of them. Their specialty was soon French literature. They reveled in Balzac, in Stendhal and Proust, and later in Gide and Sartre. But they developed a particular interest in the shorter pieces of Gallic literature such as the letters of Madame de Sévigné, of Madame du Deffand, and of Mademoiselle de Lespinasse, the maxims of La Rochefoucauld, and the precepts of Pascal. Intrigued by the brief penned portraits that Mademoiselle de Scudéry did of her contemporaries, they decided at Rosina's suggestion to try their hand at some written sketches of their own, and Kate produced one of the Misses Rhinelander, elderly sister members of the Colony Club to which Kate and Rosina both belonged. In Rosina's opinion it might have been written by Madame de Sévigné herself.

When Rosina read Kate's piece, she knew that she had embarked on a project that was going to take her friend further than Rosina had planned. She had discovered the writer in Kate, and it was very possibly going to prove the most important event of her own lifetime. After all, it had so far been a life of receiving, of appreciating, and even if such an existence was as necessary to art as creation itself, it was still not creation. It might be the ultimate satisfaction of the human state to be both.

Rosina had not decided at what point she should seriously go to work in altering her friend's way of life, but something she observed one August morning at the Southampton Beach Club made her conclude that there was no more time to be lost. Walking down the flagstone terrace that separated the clubhouse from the beach, she stopped at the sight of a small boy in bathing trunks playing in the sand. The boy was Willy Rand, one of Kate's twins.

This was hardly unusual. What was more so was that he was wearing a pair of long green rubber gloves, much too large for his hands and arms, and huge sunglasses with no glass in them, and he was playing with a snakelike red tube.

Kate came up behind her. "It's rather a quaint sight, isn't it?" she admitted.

"What is that thing he's got?" Rosina wanted to know. "It looks like an enema tube."

"I'm afraid it *is* an enema tube."

"Kate, what will the stylish members of this club think when they see *that?*"

"Not much, I fear. But you see, the child's been ill, and he gets so querulous when he doesn't have the things he wants to play with that I'm afraid he'll run a temperature."

"Better than if the club manager does. Really, Kate! I suppose this is from one of those crazy books you're always reading about the latest theories of childcare."

"Well, I do like to keep up to date. And in Dr. Bonsal's new treatise, he claims that indulging a child needn't—"

"Where's the boy's nurse?" Rosina interrupted.

"She's taking the girls swimming."

"Well, get her and tell her to take Willy to some part of the beach where he's less visible. And then come join me for a cooling drink."

Later, when the two of them were seated at an umbrella table on the terrace, Rosina decided that her moment had come.

"I've never been convinced there's a god, Kate, but if there be one, surely he, she, or it never intended that you should waste the considerable talent you've been given supplying enema tubes to children of bizarre tastes who would be far better off left to their efficient nurses. I miss my guess if God didn't intend you to write a great novel." In the silence that followed Rosina noted that Kate was interested. Perhaps even deeply interested. "Well, then, write it!"

After a moment Kate shook her head. "I might get too involved."

"Wouldn't that be just the fun of it? Even perhaps the joy of it?"

"Not, you see, Rosina, if it interfered with my principal duties."

"You mean your family, of course. But, Kate dear, your husband works all day, and your children will be more and more taken up with their schools and sports and nasty little friends. You'll have plenty of time to write."

"It's not just a question of time, Rosina. It's a question of emphasis. Howard works hard, it's true, and the older girls are more often away now, but they all still need me, and they depend on me to provide a home base where they will always be comforted, encouraged, and deeply understood. I don't for a minute undervalue my importance in their lives. And to maintain it has got to be my primary goal. Of course, I have time to do some writing. But I know myself well enough to know that if I really gave myself to an art, I'd end up giving it all I've got. There would be very little left over for anyone else."

"Well, hooray! That will be just what will save you when the children are all married, middle-aged, and moodily self-centered, and a retired Howard is living on the golf course!"

"There'll be grandchildren, I hope."

"You can't make a life out of grandchildren. They go through the expected act of 'adoring' old granny, but it doesn't mean much. I know. I was a granddaughter myself once. I remember those Sunday lunches!"

"Well, Rosina, I guess we must agree to disagree."

"Not before I've said one more thing. I know what you think of me, Kate. You're much too kind to say it to me, or indeed to anyone else, but deep down you regard me as a frustrated old maid who tries to cover her lack of a loving family in collecting bibelots and raising begonias. You imagine that I secretly envy you. And I do! But not for your spouse or your daughters or even for the little boy playing with the enema tube. No! I envy you for the talent that you're criminally wasting and that one day you will passionately regret!"

Kate was perfectly aware, in the months that followed, that her friend had undertaken a campaign to undermine her faith in the lares and penates of her domestic life with the object of clearing the field for a literary career. But she did not really mind this; indeed, she found it rather titillating. That an intellect as keen as Rosina's should deem her capable of serious writing was exciting to her. She might have no intention of abandoning the established goals of her private life, but she saw no harm in playing with the idea. It was a pleasing fantasy.

Rosina started her project by purporting to find clay feet at the base of the idol of the Rand household: the great former governor and senator Clarence Cook, who was the revered senior partner of Howard's firm. Kate had had no reason hitherto to suspect that her own deep admiration of Cook was not totally merited. He was the kind of man whom other men both liked and wanted to be. He was not only an expert lawyer and a deft administrator, he was a splendid piece of male furniture: stalwart, broad-shouldered, with thick wavy white hair, large friendly hazel-blue eyes, a commanding brow and chin, and a deep voice that was hearty and usually welcoming. And though he had an upper-class stance and manner — he came of old colonial stock — he knew just how to put humbler folk at their ease; at firm outings that included the whole staff he would spread general hilarity and share his thermos with the office boys. You couldn't fault him. At least Kate couldn't.

But Rosina could. She was a client of Anthon, Cook, and Bartlett, though her means were much slighter than those of the tycoons on their roster, because her family had been represented by the firm since its origin, and Cook was loyal to old retainers.

"But surely Clarence looks after you well," Kate protested after one of her friend's more withering remarks. "Didn't you tell me that he always sees you himself when you go to the office, and doesn't pawn you off on some junior?"

"Oh, he does that indeed, and does it very well!" Rosina exclaimed with mock enthusiasm. "I am ushered at once into his great paneled office where I sink in carpet. He rises to greet me with a beaming smile that would conceal his inner thoughts to anyone less percipient than your humble servant."

"And how do you read those inner thoughts?"

"Oh, very clearly. He is thinking, Here she is, that sad old virgin, counting on her antecedents to lower my fee. But he comforts himself with the recollection that he is only performing his god-given function of providing solace to those who must envy his fame, his glory, his goodness!"

"Oh, Rosina, you really are most unfair."

"Am I?"

Kate chose not to go on with the discussion. It made her uneasy, for she knew how great a debt her husband owed to Cook. It was the senior partner who bolstered Howard's position in the firm. Howard might be expert enough in the details of the ancient and technical laws of real estate and property and popular in the firm, but Kate knew that there were younger members, avid for higher percentages of the net income, who questioned the need of Howard's department at all or reasoned that it could be handled by a clerk, not a partner. And Kate suspected that the senior partner's distinct preference for her company at office social gatherings—like her, he was a great reader and found little congeniality with other partners' wives—was a possible asset in his continuing support of her husband.

It so happened that on the night of this last discussion of Cook with Rosina, Howard came home from the office with a very drawn look. He explained it after she had mixed him his cocktail.

"Clarence came to see me in my office today. I knew it was important for otherwise he'd have sent for me. And it *was* important. He informed me that the executive committee has decided to invite Sam Zebulon to become a member of the firm."

"I don't believe it!"

"It's true."

"Can't he overturn the committee?"

"Kate, dear, the executive committee executes only what Clarence tells them! He came to me because he knows of our connection with Zebulon."

"And did you tell him about the wretch?"

"There's very little Clarence doesn't know. But there are also things he doesn't want to know."

"Then what are you going to do about it?"

"I'm going to grin and bear it. What else?"

Sam Zebulon was an evil spirit in Howard's family. He had been a brilliant office boy in Uncle Jules Anthon's office, so able and quick that Uncle Jules had put him through law school. He had graduated first in his class and applied for a job in the firm of his benefactor. As in those days, Uncle Jules's firm had been one of the downtown groups that employed no Jews, and he had been rejected. Uncle Jules got him a job in a smaller firm, but Zebulon had apparently harbored a deep resentment that surfaced in the brutal way he handled a lawsuit against Uncle Jules's son, representing the son's alienated wife and bringing up unproven charges of child abuse and homosexuality. Zebulon had gone on to become famous for the huge awards he obtained for rather tainted spouses, and his reputation at the bar was cloudy, to say the least. But of recent years he appeared to have somewhat cleaned himself up and won fame successfully representing the thoroughly respectable and clearly wronged wife of one of the nation's richest men.

"But, darling, this will change the whole character of the firm!"

"Clarence doesn't see it that way. He says our trust and estate department needs a beefing up, and this is the man to do it. I pointed out that it's a departure from our policy of only making partners from within, but he says we haven't the right candidate within. He's not going to change his mind, so that's that."

She knew now that he would never speak again of the matter to his senior partner. Howard looked up to Clarence Cook as his god. But might she not for once try her own hand at the game? The high and unblemished reputation of the firm was certainly one of the major penates on the domestic altar at which she daily dedicated her life. And was not the senior partner her particular friend? Did he not seek out her company at office social events, even to the jealousy of some of the other partners' wives? With her he could show a side of himself not always visible to those who surrounded him: he could be the reader, the philosopher, the man whose mind leapt to the unknowable beyond the daily grind of the bar. And was he not an idealist? Could he really tolerate a conjunction with such a man as Zebulon if he were possessed of the facts? Never!

The following Sunday, when she and Howard were weekending in their Hampton villa, they were invited to a large Sunday lunch at the neighboring Cook estate. After the meal her host took her for a private stroll to view his rose garden, in which he took great pride, and she found herself seated with him on a marble bench by a fountain irrigated from the lips of carved frogs. It was her moment to speak.

Why did she suddenly think of Mrs. Samson and the dinner party she had skipped in order to take the children on a picnic? Mrs. Samson, it was true, had been a guest at the lunch, and was still in the house, but it was not that. Was it a sense that she, Kate, was not fitting into the world as it was? That she was a dingy bird without protective coloration?

Still, she proceeded.

"Howard and I, Clarence, can't help wondering if you would be so willing to make a partner of Mr. Zebulon if you knew what we know about him."

"And what is it that you know, Kate?"

Clarence had at once adopted his bland expressionless legal look. He didn't flicker an eye or utter a word while she expatiated, nervously and sometimes repetitiously, on the dark side of the man whom she finally summed up as a Uriah Heep.

When Cook spoke, it was with the faintest tinge of threat in his tone. "Did Howard put you up to this?"

"Oh, never!" she gasped. "This is just between you and me."

"Then that is just where we should leave it."

Kate hesitated. Did she catch a flash of yellow in those watching eyes? Like the distant glint of lightning on a sultry summer day? Was she approaching the limit of the little meadow specially mowed for her and Howard Rand? Was she daring to step into the dark neighboring woods that she had hitherto seen as simply romantic? But she had a job to do.

"But you must see, Clarence, that the firm is Howard's life as well as his business. It's his club, his friends, almost his family. And I wonder if he could bring himself even to speak to a man whom he regards, rightly or wrongly, as evil incarnate."

"Are you telling me, Kate, that I would have two partners who would not be on speaking terms with each other?"

"I'm afraid so, yes."

"Then it will be your job to talk Howard out of any such behavior. If Howard is to continue as my partner, it will be necessary for him to be on good terms with every other partner."

"Oh, Clarence, how can I guarantee that?"

"Because you must. For Howard's own good and that of his family. Now listen to me, Kate. I am going to tell you some home truths. Howard is a loveable man, probably the most popular of the partners with the clerks and staff. And he is a good and careful lawyer with his deeds and mortgages. In a small town, with a local practice, he would be one of the leaders of the community. But in New York he's in a league that's too big for him. If we shut down his department, as some of the partners want to, and farm out its work to a small specialized firm, there would be no other department in which I could place him. He has no expertise in corporate law or litigation, and he's not the type for either, anyway. He could probably get a job in a real estate firm, but only at a small fraction of what we now pay him. I've kept his department going, Kate, but only by using my veto in our executive committee. If I can do that for him, you can do this. Make him see the light."

It was to Kate as if she had gone up to the observation tower of a skyscraper only to have the promenade deck collapse around her, forcing her to cling to the wall. "It's going to be hard to tell him all that."

"Not as hard as you think. People are apt to know more about their tenuous hold on reality than they let on."

"But what you don't see, Clarence, is how awful it will be for Howard to learn that his position in the firm depends on your bounty. He has always liked to imagine that he is an integral part of the firm's history. That some kind of mantle, however abbreviated, had descended from his uncle Jules to his own shoulders. He tried to see the family connection as a kind of figurehead, not as a real power base, of course, but perhaps as a handy symbol of past and continuing eminence in the field of law."

"Jules Anthon is not only forgotten," Clarence pronounced roughly, "he was never much remembered. He belonged to that generation of old Knickerbocker lawyers who, with their pompous airs, could actually convince the new robber barons that they were competent counsel."

"Then Howard didn't owe his partnership to him?"

"Oh, I don't say that. In his day the old boy could be quite convincing. His only real genius was that he believed in the image he sought to cast. People were likely to do what he told them to do. It was only after he was gone that they recognized that they'd been had. Howard doesn't have that kind of brashness. He's too modest. That's why he needs you."

"To help him toe the line?"

"To make him see the world as it is."

But Kate, nodding submissively as she rose with him now to return to the house, knew that she would not have to talk to her husband of the matter at all. He would go along with the boss. As Cook had said, people know more than you think. It was to demolish her dreams that the senior partner had spoken.

The following Tuesday, back in town, she lunched with Rosina at the Colony Club. Her mind was still under the shadow that Cook had cast, and, incapable of taking much interest in any other topic, she was about to tell her friend that she would like to reconsider the latter's evaluation of Howard's senior partner when she was interrupted at her first mention of his name.

"Clarence Cook! But, my dear, it's mental telepathy! I was just about to tell you that I was in court all day yesterday listening to him cross-examine the boy's mother in that terrible custody case."

"What case is that?"

"Don't you read the newspapers? The Moberly case. Cook is representing the horrid old grandmother. No surprise. She's the one with all the money."

Kate now recalled the salient facts. Howard had spoken of it. Old Mrs. Moberly, the heiress of a Standard Oil fortune, was claiming custody of her young grandson on the grounds that her beautiful widowed daughter-in-law had been rendered an unfit mother by her promiscuous love affairs both with men and women. The daughter-in-law, in return, was demanding a settlement, as her late husband's estate, held in trust, had passed entirely to their son, leaving her penniless. The scandalous evidence submitted by the old lady's counsel had attracted wide public attention.

"You should have seen, Kate, the way Cook went after poor Daisy Moberly on cross-examination. He might have been Torquemada sending a heretic to the stake! Oh, he almost foamed at the mouth."

"But maybe she is unfit."

"Because she's taken a lover or two? If that's a crime, half the mothers we know would lose their children. And anyway we know the true reason the old bitch is after her. She's convinced that Daisy killed her worthless lush of a son by encouraging his drinking."

"And did she?"

"No! Or if she did, she was hoist by her own petard, for the money she lived on all went to the kid, and she is held to a strict accounting of every penny spent by the Surrogate's Court. The worst part of the whole business is that Daisy could have been bought off by a fraction of what this trial is costing her mother-in-law. Give her a decent allowance and the right to visit the child on certain days, and poor Daisy would grab it. And the old lady doesn't even want the boy! No! She wants to disgrace and humiliate the child's mother. And she's found just the right man to do it for her!"

"Are you being quite fair, Rosina? How can you be sure Clarence knows all this?"

"Because everyone does. Everyone who knows the Moberlys, anyway. You should have seen him in court, Kate! The apostle of virtue earning his huge virtuous fee. He dripped with venom as he implied the most disgusting things that two women might do to each other. Defense counsel was constantly objecting, of course, and the judge had to sustain him at times, but the damage had been done, and you could see that the black-robed old beetle was enjoying every minute of the filthy argument and was on Cook's side."

Kate had long suspected that Rosina might have had to struggle with sapphic urges herself, and that this might be a factor in her embracement of Daisy Moberly's cause. She had no prejudice against lesbianism except that it stood in the way of what she considered a woman's primary function: to give birth.

"You don't think, Rosina, that in representing his client Cook should use every legal weapon at hand?"

"There you go, Kate, sticking up for anyone who has anything to do with Howard's sacred firm. But let me tell you, they're not all like Howard. I sometimes wonder if they don't resent our sex in their hearts. When a beautiful and loveable woman like Daisy Moberly dares to do what she chooses with her own body, when she has the courage to seek love with someone a little more caring than her drunken impotent lord and master, she must be stripped of her offspring and crucified in the gutter press!"

"If she'd only been a little more discreet about it—"

"Oh, don't give me that, Kate! Cook had detectives trailing her. I heard their testimony!"

Kate suddenly felt she could take no more of this. She rose from the table. "Rosina, I have a terrible headache. I'm going home."

"Oh, you poor dear! And here I've been yakking away like nothing. Let me take you home."

"No, no, it's not that bad. I'll take a couple of aspirins and lie down."

She shook herself free of her protesting friend and took a taxi home. All the children were at school, and she was able to pull down the shades in her bedroom and be, blessedly, alone. She kept saying one word over and over to herself as she lay in her bed staring up at the ceiling. *Vastation.* She was having a vastation. She had read the word in a book about Henry James, Sr. He had felt the presence of evil squatting in a corner. So had she.

When Rosina called at the house the next morning to reassure herself that her friend's complaint had been nothing worse than a headache, she found her sitting alone and seemingly desolate in the living room without even a book in her lap. The children were at school, Howard at his office, and the place was silent except for the hum of a vacuum cleaner on the floor above.

"Are you all right, dear?"

Kate looked up at her blankly for a moment before answering. "Quite all right." Her tone was flat.

"Headache gone?"

"I didn't have one."

Rosina pulled up a chair now and seated herself beside Kate. "Kate, dear, what's the matter?"

There was another pause. "Everything. I seem to have lost my taste."

"Taste for what?"

"Well, for life, for one. When the girls came home from school yesterday, I found I couldn't face the usual half-hour of reading aloud to them before their supper. So I told them to get on with their homework. And when Howard came in I hardly heard him at dinner when he told me about his day.

He thought I must be just tired, and later he played soothing records for me. But I didn't care. I didn't care at all."

"Maybe you were just tired."

"It was more than that, Rosina. I saw my whole world differently. The colors had all run. I saw that I had idealized Howard's run-of-the-mill law firm, that I had turned a blind eye to their greed for fees. That I had overestimated Howard's contribution to it, that he simply hung on at the mercy of Cook. And that his famous uncle was a myth. I even began to see my children—"

"Oh, Kate, no!" Rosina interrupted.

"Oh, it was nothing really bad, the poor dears. I simply saw the girls being prepared for a life as dull as my own and the boy for one as dim as his dad's. Howard and I were duplicating ourselves, that was all."

Rosina was pensive for some moments. When she spoke her tone was decisive. "Perhaps this is a blessing in disguise. Perhaps this is the moment at last when you must make a change in your life."

"How?"

"You might start by putting down on paper exactly what has happened to you. You know I've always seen you as a writer."

"But I don't want to write about myself. That's my trouble. I'm sick and tired of myself."

"Then write a novel! A *Madame Bovary*. Wasn't she stifled and bored?"

"You want me, recovering from a vision of life as *Little Women*, to leap right into the shoes of Flaubert?"

"Something like that. Why not? What can you lose, anyway, by trying?"

Kate refused to go on with the subject, but when her friend had left, she found herself giving it a good deal of serious thought, and when Howard came home that night she asked him to tell her about the progress of the Moberly case. Pleased to see her interest in things reignited, he spoke of it at some length, extolling the wonderful effectiveness of Clarence Cook's aggressive tactics.

The next day she asked Rosina if she could attend the trial with her, and the two spent the whole day in a courtroom in Foley Square, listening to Daisy Moberly's desperate lawyer attempt to whitewash his lovely client. In the taxi home Kate felt an idea explode in her mind, covering her whole being with its golden flashes.

She said nothing to her friend, but the whole next day she worked on an outline of a novel, and before a week had passed she was writing it. She devoted her mornings to it as soon as the children had left for school, and she corrected her drafts in the afternoon. She excused herself from all other engagements, but she devoted her evenings to her family. And she found that her good moods had returned; she was happy, even exuberant. Howard was delighted to hear of her new occupation and begged to be allowed to read the work in progress. But Kate would not allow that. She was afraid he would object to her source material.

For her book was based on the Moberly case. This would surely have bothered Howard, but it did not bother her. She had learned in her readings with Rosina that some novelists had to draw from life and others from their imagination. Every character of Charlotte Brontë's fiction could be traced to someone she knew; none of Emily's. Well, she was a Charlotte, that was all.

But the picture she was drawing was considerably darker than the one presented by the case. The grandmother was turned into an embittered old woman who had been married for her money and had subconsciously taken her revenge on the man who had never returned her misguided love by spoiling and indulging the weak son he adored until the latter succumbed to gambling and alcohol. When her son committed suicide, she couldn't face such evidence of her own folly and convinced herself that his wife had driven him to it. The wife, however, is no better than her mother-in-law; she cares little for her young boy and is primarily interested in attaining control of his money to continue her promiscuous round of pleasure. The lawyers on both sides are seen as heating up the controversy to swell their fees, and the judge is intent on giving the scandalous aspects of the case the widest publicity to bring his own name before the voters and enhance his chances for appointment to a higher court. The only pure character is the little boy, who like the eponymous heroine of James's *What Maisie Knew*, is well aware that he is only a pawn in the battle of titans.

The book was finished in three months.

"Of course, I've made the case much blacker than it is," she admitted to Rosina, to whom alone she had submitted the manuscript. "The facts aren't nearly so bad."

"How do you know that? You may have hit them right on the head. But that's not the point. All the things you describe exist in our society. Like Dostoyevsky you have chosen a dramatic way to drive your point home. Kate, you've written a great novel!"

Kate clasped her hands in ecstasy. She had never imagined such a tide of joy. "But I can't publish it," she murmured unconvincingly.

"If you don't, I'll disown you forever!"

Howard had to be shown the book. She gave it to him on a Saturday morning, and he read it all day. When he joined her that evening for a cocktail and handed her back the manuscript, his face was grave.

"Well?" she asked with a beating heart.

"It's a great story. It's stunning, really. It almost scares me that you could have written it. It's a shock for me to discover there's that much of you I've never known."

"You mean you've married a monster?" She tried to smile.

"No. That I've got a wife who can create them."

"And what can I do with my monsters?"

"You can put them in print."

"You mean I should try to publish the book?"

"You should try and you'll surely succeed. I miss my guess if we don't have a bestseller on our hands."

"But, darling, what about your firm? How will they react?"

"Oh, they won't like it at all. We must face that."

"But if it hurts your career . . . ?"

"It will start yours," he finished for her. "And yours will be the better one."

She rose to hug him. "You're the most generous man I ever knew!"

Some successes are years in coming; many come too late. Kate's seemed to come overnight. Rosina talked a famous literary agent into reading the book; he was immediately taken with it and had no difficulty in selling it to a well-known and enthusiastic publishing house. A happy Kate was checking galleys one morning at home when she had an unexpected visitor.

It was rare for the older Mrs. Rand to call on her daughter-in-law; the latter was expected to come to her on certain Sunday lunches. She and Kate had never been congenial, but she had had to recognize that Kate had done more with Howard than his mother had been able to and that she had been a good mother. They were formally on good terms. But the grim look the old lady gave her daughter-in-law as she slowly seated herself did not augur a pleasant interview.

"Howard has told me the subject of this novel you're bringing out, Kate. He says that it deals with a custody case similar to one handled by his office."

"Some of my incidents may have been suggested by the case, yes."

"Howard implied there was more to it than that. The reason he told me was that I should be prepared for some trouble at the office. As you well know, it was my brother's firm, and Mr. Cook has always handled my affairs personally."

"Mrs. Rand, there are always going to be people who cannot conceive that a novelist has any imagination at all. They think every character, every incident in a novel is directly copied from something in the author's own life. If we writers worried about that, there'd be no novels at all."

Mrs. Rand's slightly raised eyebrows implied that this was an eventuality with which she could live. "I asked Howard what he would do if the firm held him responsible for any repercussions arising from the publication of your book."

"Oh, Mrs. Rand, they wouldn't be so petty!"

"Wouldn't they? Do you know what Howard told me?"

Kate frowned. "No. What?"

"He said he could always resign."

"But that's absurd!"

"But are you willing to take the chance? Are you willing to risk your husband's career for the satisfaction of publishing one story? Of course you're not! You can always write another, can't you?"

Kate sat up very straight. She was suddenly ready for the crisis. "It's not that easy, Mrs. Rand. I may be a one-book author, and this may be my one book. But I'm going to publish it, and nothing is going to stop me. You talk about your son's career. What about mine? This book is my life!"

"Then you're a very selfish woman! Even more than I've always suspected!"

"You call *me* selfish! You, who have subjected your family to every whim of a *malade imaginaire!*"

Mrs. Rand stood slowly. "I got your husband his job through my brother. You will have cost him it through your silly book. Which is the more selfish?"

And she turned to the door.

———

Kate's novel enjoyed a critical and popular success. She even sold it to the movies for a sum far greater than Howard could earn in years. This was just as well, as Howard, having incurred the expressed reprobation of his partners over the caricature of Clarence Cook in Kate's book and the loss of old Mrs. Moberly's retainer, suffered a nervous breakdown that was certainly a factor in his ultimately seeking early retirement. Kate's ample earnings from later books adequately supported her family. She was not a one-book author.

She did not, however, go unscathed. Thelma, her oldest girl, became something of a rebel in her freshman year at New York University. Like many a teenager, she sought in her mother the source of anything in her life that troubled her, and, as her kind father was a vulnerable being, she joined him to herself as victims of the maternal malevolence.

"You bought your literary fame at the cost of Dad's happiness," she threw in Kate's face. "You walked over his stricken body to grab your laurels!"

Kate simply smiled. "What a lovely time you're having, dear. And, of course, what you're saying is perfectly true. But you leave out the fact that I was fighting for my life. Your father had had his. I wanted mine. And I got it. And at least I have the honesty to make no excuses. I'd do the same thing again if I had it to do over. And like it or not, my dear, there's a good bit of me in you."

THE COUNTRY COUSIN
A Comedy in One Act

DRAMATIS PERSONAE
(In order of appearance)

MRS. NELLIE HONE

ELIDA RODMAN, *her niece*

ALICE, *a maid*

CAROLINE HONE, *Mrs. Hone's daughter-in-law*

ALEXANDER HONE, *Mrs. Hone's son*

WINTHROP DELANCEY

MISS EMILY HARCROSSE

MISS HARRIET HARCROSSE, *Emily's sister*

SCENE 1: *Living room of Mrs. Hone's apartment on upper Park Avenue, New York. Late on a weekday afternoon, autumn 1937.*

SCENE 2: *Same, one hour later.*

SCENE 3: *Same, five hours later.*

174

ACT I

Scene 1

TIME: *Late on a weekday afternoon, autumn 1937*
PLACE: *The living room of MRS. HONE's apartment on upper Park Avenue, New York. It is an old building and an old room. In the center is a threshold with double doors opening into the vestibule. At stage R. is a door leading to the dining room, at stage L. to a den. The wall to the left of door C. is covered almost to the ceiling with bookcases, and masses of books, large, old, presumably valuable, are jammed into their shelves, with magazines and papers stuffed on top of them. On top of the bookcase is the marble bust of a Roman emperor and several bronzes, an Antinous, a satyr pursuing a nymph, a chariot, etc. To upstage R. is a magnificent Sheraton sideboard with silver pitchers and decanters. The wall above it is covered with paintings in heavy gilt frames, a Bouguereau angel, some chess-playing cardinals, Christians in the arena, a girl with her dog. The furniture is a mixture of heavy Victorian with some rather nice Empire and English eighteenth century; it represents, like everything else, accumulation rather than collection. One feels that the owner is sentimental, but not tasteless, that each bit of bric-a-brac and each of the framed photographs that clutter the tables cannot be sacrificed.*
AT CURTAIN: *MRS. HONE and ELIDA RODMAN are seated opposite each other. MRS. HONE is seated in what is apparently her usual armchair, a huge leather affair near door R., beside a table covered with bibelots, which she idly fingers. ELIDA is reading aloud to her. She is pale and thin, with long black hair, about twenty-nine, and one feels from her tired expression and simple dark dress that she is a sort of dependent relative or companion. MRS. HONE, a large, stout woman, has a round, intelligent,*

immobile face, the face of a woman of high blood pressure and high temper and pronounced opinions. She wears a pince-nez and is dressed in the commodious, styleless comfort of the semi-invalid.

ELIDA (*Reading*): "The men who replaced the Neanderthalers, while using the caves and shelters of their predecessors, lived largely in the open. They were hunting peoples who hunted the mammoth and wild horse as well as the reindeer and bison. Unlike most savage conquerors, who take the women of the defeated for their own and interbreed with them, it would seem that these true men would have nothing whatever to do with the Neanderthalers. They lived on a new and greater level, and with them we trace, on their walls and on their rude implements, the dawn of self-expression."

MRS. HONE (*Holding up a piece of ivory that she has picked up from the table at her side*): It's from the tusk of a mammoth, you know, Elida. Somewhere in the steppes of Russia in the early Paleolithic. (*Dreamily*) That early air was the air we were meant to breathe. Alexander and I.

ELIDA (*Looking at the book in her lap*): I don't see Alexander being very happy in Russia.

MRS. HONE (*Sternly*): I was speaking prehistorically, of course. He's a good boy, my Alexander.

ELIDA (*With just a hint of correction*): A good son, Aunt Nellie.

MRS. HONE: How many sons do you know who would go to see their old mother every afternoon of the autumn, winter, and spring?

ELIDA: Very few, I'm afraid.

MRS. HONE: Few? Do you know *any?*

ELIDA (*Giving in*): No, I don't suppose I know any, Aunt Nellie.

MRS. HONE (*Regarding her suspiciously*): Every afternoon, rain or shine, on his way from the bank. But perhaps you think it isn't entirely on *my* account that he pays his visits. Is that it, Elida?

ELIDA (*Surprised*): Why, no, Aunt Nellie. Of course not. Why else would he possibly come?

MRS. HONE (*With a touch of bitterness*): Why else indeed? How should *I* know?

ELIDA (*Shrugging*): You surely don't think he comes to see his old maid cousin?

MRS. HONE (*Reprovingly*): You're too young to speak of yourself as an old maid. I've warned you about that.

ELIDA: It's a state of mind, not of age. But all right. You surely don't think he comes to see his mother's companion?

MRS. HONE: And I particularly asked you not to speak of yourself as my companion. You happen to be my niece.

ELIDA: But you pay me.

MRS. HONE: Of course I pay you. You can't live on air, can you?

ELIDA: Your daughter-in-law seems to think so. She treats me like a servant.

MRS. HONE (*Snorting*): Caroline treats us *all* like servants. She always has.

ELIDA: But it's different with you. She resents you. We at least respect the people we resent.

MRS. HONE (*Rather pleased*): I knew she disliked me. I didn't know she resented me. Why should she resent me?

ELIDA: Because Alexander's so fond of you. I suppose it's only natural for her.

MRS. HONE (*Sarcastic*): Of course! We all have to bow now to the principle that a husband and wife belong entirely to each other. If he happens to like his own mother, oh, that's bad. *That's* domination. (*Snorts*) Small wonder there's so much divorce.

ELIDA: Did I tell you she's coming in this afternoon?

MRS. HONE: Who?

ELIDA: Caroline.

MRS. HONE (*Irritated*): But they're dining here tonight. And you know I have to rest before *Tristan*. What do you suppose I keep you for, child?

ELIDA: I'm sorry. She said it was important.

MRS. HONE: Oh, she did, did she? *Now* what do you suppose I've done?

ELIDA: I have no idea. But we'll find out soon enough.

MRS. HONE (*Sighing*): Yes. And if I don't see her, she'll take it out on my poor boy. That's the devil of in-laws. They always have a hostage. Well, we may as well get on with the chapter. Perhaps we can finish it before she comes.

ELIDA (*Closing the book with her finger holding her place*): Aunt Nellie?

MRS. HONE: Yes, child?

ELIDA: Can I ask you something?

MRS. HONE: Why not?

ELIDA: Would you mind so terribly if I went home? For a while?

MRS. HONE (*Alert*): A while? How long a while?

ELIDA: Well . . . maybe quite a while.

MRS. HONE (*Hostile*): What's wrong? Don't you like New York?

ELIDA: Oh, yes, of course, I love it, and you've been terribly kind, but I think Mummy may need me in Augusta.

MRS. HONE: Your mother need you? With seven other children in that box of a house? Are you out of your mind? She's tickled to death to have you here.

ELIDA: But there are all sorts of things I could do. I—

MRS. HONE (*Interrupting firmly*): Nonsense. There are plenty of helping hands up there. I told your mother when she married that she might as well have lots of children. In the walk of life that *she* had chosen they can be assets.

ELIDA: But you don't need me, Aunt Nellie. I mean you could get a *real* companion who would dress you and make up your medicines.

MRS. HONE (*Sternly*): A "real" companion? Is *this* my reward for putting you through college, Elida Rodman?

ELIDA (*Hanging her head*): Oh, no.

MRS. HONE: Is *this* what I get in return for the checks I've sent your mother every Christmas day these past thirty years? Do you know what those checks have meant to her?

ELIDA: I'm sorry, Aunt Nellie.

MRS. HONE (*Snorting*): A "real" companion, indeed! So that's all you thought of the operas we've been to together, the books we've read aloud. And I was thinking, like an old fool, that I might have given you at least some inkling of the function of beauty in life, some conception of what— oh, what's the use? (*She breaks off, shaking her head.*)

ELIDA: But you *have*. Really, you have.

MRS. HONE: And now you want to bury yourself in Augusta, perhaps even marry a hotel proprietor the way your mother did? (*ELIDA says nothing.*) Well, go ahead, then! I'm not stopping you.

ELIDA (*Quietly*): I won't go if you disapprove, Aunt Nellie. I know all you've done for my family.

MRS. HONE: All I've *done!* I'll have none of that, young lady. You'll pawn off no shabby gratitude on me. Either there's human love and affection or there's not, but gratitude, bah! I have no room for gratitude.

(*Sound of the front doorbell*)

MRS. HONE: Caroline! (*Shifting into brogue, with the heavy humor of her kind of eccentric*) Oh, me trials and tribulations! Bring me some whiskey, child. I can't face *her* on a parched whistle.

(*ALICE, an ancient maid, appears, crossing the hall in back, and a moment later CAROLINE HONE enters briskly. She is thin and chic, but the effect is spoiled by the angularity of her features and the arrogant condescension of her manner.*)

CAROLINE: Elida, I wonder if you'd be a dear and get me a touch of whiskey on the rocks? I've had such a day, and tea wouldn't start to do the trick. Besides, I have a bone to pick with your aunt. (*Nods at MRS. HONE with a little smirk*) And that takes *something.*

(*ELIDA moves to the sideboard to get and deliver the whiskey to CAROLINE and MRS. HONE during the following dialogue. CAROLINE crosses the room to sit by her mother-in-law, whom she addresses with the insulting cheerfulness of one speaking to a child.*)

And how are we feeling, Mrs. Hone? All ready for the big outing tonight? Pretty spiky? Oh, I'll bet you are!

MRS. HONE (*Glaring at her*): I'm never spiky, as you put it, Caroline. There are evenings such as tonight, when the prospect of beautiful music induces me, unwisely perhaps, to venture abroad.

CAROLINE (*Taking off her gloves*): Unwisely, fiddlesticks. I'm sure it's the best thing in the world for you. But I didn't come here to discuss that, Mrs. Hone. That's a matter for your doctors, of whom Lord knows there are plenty. But there's another matter I'd like to take up with you, if you don't mind. A slightly more serious one.

MRS. HONE: Bless me! Shall the old be listened to?

CAROLINE (*In a clear, sarcastic tone that nonetheless betrays nervousness*): I want to find out, Mrs. Hone, whether you, like myself, have had any reason to suspect that Alexander has recently been finding the company of some other woman more attractive than mine.

MRS. HONE (*Staring*): Some *other* woman?

CAROLINE (*Sourly sweet*): By which I am not, of course, referring to yourself, whose company, I well know, he prefers to all others.

MRS. HONE (*Angry*): He's a good son, Caroline. A faithful son. Are you going to make *that* a fault now?

CAROLINE: Hardly. That's a battle I lost years ago. No, I'm referring to a possible girlfriend. A rival of both of ours, if you care to put it that way.

MRS. HONE (*Her jaw forward, still glaring at CAROLINE*): I don't care to put it any way, Caroline. Must you discuss such things before this child here?

CAROLINE (*Throwing ELIDA, who is handing CAROLINE her drinks, a brief glance*): Oh, Elida. She knows all our secrets. Don't you, Elida? I'd like to have her opinion, too. (*ELIDA glances around nervously and walks over to the bookcase.*)

MRS. HONE: I should think you'd be ashamed to have others know!

CAROLINE: Ashamed? Me? And what about your precious Alexander?

MRS. HONE (*Picking up the piece of ivory, again in her dreamy tone*): I was showing this to Elida. Before you came in. It's from the tusk of a mammoth. Early Paleolithic. That's something you haven't guessed about us Hones, Caroline. For all your shrewdness.

CAROLINE: There's very little I haven't guessed about Alexander. What is it that I haven't guessed about the Hones?

MRS. HONE: That we're Paleolithics.

CAROLINE: You're *what*? (*Irritated, as she takes it in as only another manifestation of Mrs. Hone's heavy eccentricity*) Oh. Well, I'm glad I don't have to depend on Alexander's hunting, if that's what you mean.

MRS. HONE (*Loftily*): Alexander and I were never ones to love our fetters. If he has put aside his slingshot and is visiting the priestess of a neighboring village, is it up to his old mother, whose love of freedom he inherits, to give him away? Don't worry, Caroline. Alexander will always return to his cave.

CAROLINE (*Bleakly*): Well, when he does, he'll find that I haven't put aside *my* slingshot. Or my small stone hatchet.

MRS. HONE (*Moving to the offensive*): Why do you suspect my boy? What are your grounds?

CAROLINE (*Coolly*): My grounds, as you might imagine in such a case, are utterly inadequate. For instance, this summer, when I was away at the Cape with the children, I heard that he was seen dining at a restaurant in the city, in a corner, with a dark-haired girl who kept turning her face away from the room.

(ELIDA suddenly looks around in consternation. She turns quickly back to the bookshelves.)

And the other day when I was going through the pockets of a suit of his that I was sending to the cleaner's I found two used ticket stubs for the Lincoln Theatre. That's where *The Ballad Girl* is playing. I told him that night that I wanted to see it and asked him if by any chance he'd been. He said no. *(After a pause, significantly)* He said he was dying to.

MRS. HONE: You call that evidence?

ELIDA: A very little goes a long way with a man as stuffy as Alexander.

MRS. HONE: He couldn't have forgotten going to a musical comedy?

CAROLINE: Hardly. When he was still *dying* to see it.

MRS. HONE *(Sternly)*: It could be that he doesn't find his own cave as enticing as it might be. It *could* be that he's not the only one at fault.

CAROLINE: Oh, of course. Anyone but your darling boy!

MRS. HONE: Look into your own heart, Caroline. Search there.

CAROLINE *(Exploding)*: *My* heart! How can you defend him, Mrs. Hone? Of course, if you think keeping some little slut in a love nest, presumably with *my* money, is Paleolithic, I don't suppose there's any point in our discussing it. To me it's disgusting.

MRS. HONE: You may think me an immoral old woman, Caroline, because I don't go around calling everything I see disgusting. There's nothing disgusting under the sky. There are only things that are beautiful. *(Meaningfully)* And things that are *not* beautiful.

CAROLINE: I wonder if you would have taken an attitude quite so philosophic while Mr. Hone was alive. Was he in the habit of paying visits to priestesses in neighboring villages?

MRS. HONE (*Shocked*): Caroline! De mortuis!

CAROLINE: Oh. I beg your pardon. That, I take it, was one of the things that was *not* beautiful.

MRS. HONE: When I had trouble I handled it myself. I didn't go about the town advertising my shame.

CAROLINE (*Getting up*): I take it from that that there *is* some shame to advertise. In your opinion, anyway. Who is this girl, Mrs. Hone?

MRS. HONE (*Closing her eyes and shaking her head*): I see nothing. I hear nothing.

CAROLINE: Is it someone I know?

MRS. HONE (*Her eyes still closed*): I hear nothing. I see nothing.

CAROLINE (*Grim*): Well, at least we know where we stand. And at least I've found out there *is* someone. We're dining with you tonight, I believe?

(*MRS. HONE simply nods.*)

And then to the opera? What is it to be?

MRS. HONE (*Murmuring*): Tristan.

CAROLINE (*Smiling ironically*): How appropriate. Till then.

(*Exit CAROLINE door C.*)

MRS. HONE (*Reaching her hand out toward ELIDA*): Give me a hand, dear. I want to go to my room.

(*With ELIDA's assistance MRS. HONE struggles to her feet.*)

Whew! That girl's visits are always bad news, but this one has laid me flat. I'll need more than my usual nap this evening, Elida. You can bring me another nip of Scotch.

To warm my blood. (*Raising her hand suddenly to her brow*)
And she's coming for dinner, too! Oh, me trials and tribulations!

ELIDA (*Anxiously*): You didn't believe what she said, Aunt
Nellie? It couldn't be true, could it?

MRS. HONE (*Giving her a sidelong look*): How should I know?
She doesn't know *who*, if that's what you're worried about.
She hasn't even a suspicion. Your old aunt was a lady from
start to finish. Don't you think?

ELIDA (*Staring*): Do *you* know, Aunt Nellie?

MRS. HONE (*Mimicking her*): Do *I* know, Aunt Nellie? What
do you suppose, my little innocent? Do you think having
eyes, I see not? Of course, I know. I know that me pride
and joy, the only issue, shall we put it, of this old body,
has left the straight and narrow at the behest of a certain
young lady. And vicee-versee.

ELIDA (*Aghast*): And who is this certain young lady, Aunt
Nellie?

MRS. HONE (*With a mocking air of astonishment*): Who indeed? Who, I wonder? Oh, Caroline doesn't know, I grant
you. But then, she's stupid. She can't see what's under her
nose. And I won't tell her, either. Never fear. But *I* know.
And you know, too, you foxy creature. Who's the little
baggage that's been waiting so shamelessly in the front
hall to tempt my virtuous boy whenever he comes to call
on his old sick mother? Who's that, I'd like to know?

ELIDA (*Her hands on her cheeks*): Aunt Nellie! It's not true!

MRS. HONE: Pish, tush.

ELIDA (*Wildly*): It's not true! It's not!

MRS. HONE (*Snorting*): Neither do I have pains in my joints.
Neither is *Tristan* a beautiful opera.

ELIDA: But we're *cousins*, Aunt Nellie. Alexander has never been anything more than kind and considerate to me.

MRS. HONE: Do you keep pictures of *all* your cousins on your dressing table?

ELIDA (*Appalled*): Aunt Nellie! You were in my room!

MRS. HONE: Certainly I was in your room. Aren't you my business, child?

ELIDA (*Suddenly passionate*): But you had no right! That's *my* room! The only place in the world that I can call my own. I must have one place that's private . . . can't you see that? (*She sinks down on the sofa and covers her face with her hands for a moment. Then she looks up and, after a moment, shrugs.*) It was only a silly picture that a photographer snapped on Broadway and sold us for fifty cents. I kept it as a souvenir.

MRS. HONE: Broadway? So it *was* you at the theater, after all. Oh, my prophetic soul, I knew it! (*She sits down heavily beside ELIDA and puts her arm around her shoulders.*) My child, you don't think I'm angry with you, do you? Or that I disapprove? You don't think your poor old aunt has gone over to the philistines? That she'd take Caroline's side? Oh, Elida. Look at me, child.

(*ELIDA looks away.*)

"To love and be so loved, yet so mistaken." Look at your old aunt and tell her all about it.

ELIDA (*Shaking her head*): But there's nothing to tell.

MRS. HONE: Oh, nothing, is that it? You talked about nothing when you dined together, when you went to the theater together, when you came home in the dark in a taxi?

ELIDA (*Indignant*): But that wasn't the way it was, Aunt Nellie! Not at all. Alexander took me out to dinner exactly once, the same evening he took me to the theater. Someone at the bank had given him tickets that afternoon, and Caroline was away. There wasn't *time* to get anyone but me.

MRS. HONE: Funny he should have lied to her about it.

ELIDA: But you know how jealous she is!

MRS. HONE: And I suppose he doesn't sit up here and talk to you after you've bundled me off to bed.

ELIDA (*Trying her best to be patient*): He sometimes sits and finishes his drink, yes. Why not? Isn't he my own first cousin?

MRS. HONE (*Grunting*): Cousin? As if that had anything to do with the price of eggs. (*Sound of doorbell again*) That's probably him now. (*Getting up slowly*) I'll ask him. We'll see if he tries to pull the wool over his poor old mother's eyes.

ELIDA (*Frantic*): Oh, Aunt Nellie, for God's sake, please! Do you want to embarrass me to death? Now, please, it's time for your rest. I'll send him right in as soon as you're ready.

MRS. HONE (*Shrugging*): All right, dear, all right. I know when I'm not wanted. (*Almost with a leer*) When the young have to be alone! (*She goes to door C. Mocking*) Oh, Caroline! if you *only knew!*

(*Exit MRS. HONE door C.*)

(*ELIDA covers her face for a moment after her aunt has gone and then, recovering, turns to door C. as ALEXANDER HONE enters. He is a medium-size man, somewhat under forty, dressed soberly and carefully in brown, his tie tied in a tiny knot. He is handsome in a mild, smooth, round-faced fashion and has the cautious, occasionally sly affability of the conscientious if not totally convinced conformist. One feels that his resistance, if any, would spring from irritability rather than anger.*)

ALEXANDER: Good evening, Elida.

ELIDA (*Tense*): Have you forgot you're dining here tonight? In an hour? Don't you have to go home and dress?

ALEXANDER (*His hand on his forehead*): God, I'd forgotten all about it. *Tristan* for four bloody hours. I'd better beat it. How's Ma?

ELIDA: Fine.

ALEXANDER (*Looking at his watch*): Maybe I have time for one drink. (*Sighs*) It's been a long day.

ELIDA (*Hesitating*): Alexander?

ALEXANDER: Yes?

ELIDA: Can I ask you something first? Something rather personal?

ALEXANDER (*Amused*): Shoot.

ELIDA (*Blurting it out*): Why didn't you tell Caroline that you'd taken me to the theater?

ALEXANDER (*After a pause*): How do you know I didn't?

ELIDA: She was here just now. She's found the ticket stubs. And she's livid. Really!

ALEXANDER (*Pursing his lips*): So that's why she's been so persnickety lately. Does she know who it was?

ELIDA: No. She came to ask your mother if *she* knew.

ALEXANDER: And did she?

ELIDA (*Hesitating*): Yes. But she didn't tell.

ALEXANDER (*Smiling as he takes this in*): Good old Ma. Oh, Elida, this could be quite a lark, you know!

ELIDA (*Upset at his attitude*): But why didn't *you* tell her?

ALEXANDER (*Changing his tone, surprised*): Why? Do you think I have to tell her every time I step out with a pretty girl?

ELIDA (*Appalled*): But you *know* it wasn't like that! You know it was perfectly innocent!

ALEXANDER (*Raising his eyebrows*): Do I? Speak for yourself.

ELIDA (*Horrified*): Alexander! What are you saying?

ALEXANDER (*Shrugging*): Simply that when I take a pretty girl out to dinner and the theater, it may be many things, but I hope it's not innocent. Good Lord, how old do you think I am?

ELIDA (*Stepping back*): Oh!

ALEXANDER (*Taking the offensive*): Well, would you really prefer it was innocent?

ELIDA: I?

ALEXANDER (*Moving a step closer to her*): Would you really rather I looked upon you as Mother's little helper? Would that be more gratifying?

ELIDA (*Staring; in a low, reproachful voice*): What must you *think* of me?

ALEXANDER: What must you think of *me*? (*Insinuatingly*) Never as a friend? A warm friend? (*Coming closer*) One who might like to be warmer?

ELIDA (*Throwing up her hands*): Alexander! What about your wife?

ALEXANDER (*Smiling broadly*): But that's just the beauty of it, don't you see? Right under her nose and she'd never guess! Never in a million years!

ELIDA: And you think I'd allow myself to drop to—*that?*

ALEXANDER: Now don't tell me you're going to go prudish on me. I know what girls are like. It's all an act with them. I thought you at least were above hypocrisy.

ELIDA (*Desperate*): Will you go now? *Please?*

ALEXANDER (*In a coaxing tone*): Oh, come off, Elida. After all, it's all in the family. (*He seizes her hand and tries to pull her to him.*)

ELIDA (*In horror*): Oh! (*She disengages herself furiously and rushes from the stage by door C. ALEXANDER shrugs and walks to the table with the whiskey decanter, which he is picking up as the curtain falls.*)

Scene 2

SCENE: Same, an hour later

AT RISE: ELIDA is alone, dressed in a simple brown evening dress, moving about the room, arranging ashtrays, fixing flowers, doing the necessary before a dinner party. ALICE enters door C.

ALICE: Mr. DeLancey, Miss Elida.

ELIDA: Oh, thank you, Alice.

(*Exit ALICE, and enter WINTHROP DELANCEY, in evening clothes, a tall, slender, distinguished man, in his early forties, with thin, receding hair combed straight back from his temples, a slightly hooked nose, and clear eyes that stare at one with a calm, semicurious detachment.*)

WINTHROP: Good evening, my dear Elida. I'm afraid I'm a bit early.

ELIDA: Oh, but I hoped you would be, Winthrop. I got ready early just in case.

WINTHROP: Well, a man couldn't ask for a better welcome than that, could he?

(*They both sit. ELIDA leans forward, clasping her hands, nervous.*)

ELIDA: There's something I wanted to talk to you about. I don't know if you know it, but . . . (*Shyly*) Well, you're really the one person around here to whom I can talk.

WINTHROP: Dear me, I hope that isn't so. I should have thought Cousin Nellie would have had a great deal to say—

ELIDA (*Interrupting*): Oh, Aunt Nellie's been very kind. It's not that. But you know how she is.

(*They exchange an understanding look.*)

And her friends. And this room! (*She looks about and gives a little shudder.*) Sometimes when I look around at the accumulated piles of opera programs, the old coins, the bits of seashell, all those huge art books so jammed in the shelves, *and* the statuettes . . . (*She sighs.*) Well, it seems almost like a great heap of bones. The aftermath of a life devoted too fiercely to devouring art and relics. As if, in the end, even discrimination has gone, and a buttonhook is the same as a Botticelli.

WINTHROP (*Sympathetic*): What William James called the inertly sentimental condition?

ELIDA (*Eagerly*): Well, isn't it? Isn't that just what it is?

WINTHROP (*Shrugging*): You should know far better than I. Cousin Nellie is your aunt. She's only my cousin by marriage.

ELIDA: But you're her lawyer. Don't lawyers have to know everything about their clients?

WINTHROP: Well, she's considerably less sentimental, I can assure you, when it comes to business. If that's what you mean.

ELIDA (*Getting up and walking restlessly about*): I wonder if it wouldn't be a nicer world the other way around.

WINTHROP: How do you mean?

ELIDA: If people were more realistic about the arts and more sentimental in business.

WINTHROP: People have their responsibilities, you know.

ELIDA (*Nodding rather sadly*): Don't I know. Uncle Robert Hone used to talk a great deal about his responsibilities.

As a child I used to think of them as the small gold objects that dangled on his watch chain which he was always fingering. (*She turns back to him with a shrug.*) Now Alexander wears them on his.

WINTHROP (*Smiling*): You're very cynical tonight.

ELIDA: I feel cynical.

WINTHROP: Has anything happened?

ELIDA (*Eagerly*): Yes, something has happened. It's what I'm trying to tell you.

WINTHROP: Is it so difficult?

ELIDA: I find it so. Because I keep thinking there are two yous. The Winthrop who's always been kind enough to listen to my petty problems, and the Winthrop who's Aunt Nellie's lawyer. Who belongs to all those clubs.

WINTHROP: Nonsense. There's only one, and he's your friend. Now go sit on the sofa and turn your back to me. You'll find it's easier that way.

ELIDA (*Doing as he says*): Does this really help? I'll try. (*A pause*) Maybe it would be easier if I started with *them*.

WINTHROP: Them?

ELIDA: Aunt Nellie and Alexander. And Caroline, too, of course. (*After a pause*) You see, when I first came here to live, I assumed, with all the self-pity of a poor relative, that they had everything. (*With a sweeping gesture*) Everything in the whole world that they could possibly want. And I, of course, had nothing. Nothing, that is, that *they* could want. It was a question, as Elizabeth Barrett Browning would have put it, of the chrism being on their head, on mine the dew.

WINTHROP: I see.

ELIDA: And then suddenly . . . well, it's hard to describe. It was rather like a nightmare. Instead of hovering in the wings as the pale and shadowy companion, it seems . . . now promise me you won't laugh, Winthrop?

WINTHROP (*Quietly*): You know I won't laugh.

ELIDA: Well, it seems I'm the leading lady.

WINTHROP: The leading lady?

ELIDA: It's as if the curtain has suddenly gone up and there I am, caught alone before a glare of lights, utterly unprepared, not a line in my head, with Alexander and Aunt Nellie and Caroline sitting out there in front, clapping their hands and stamping their feet for me to begin.

WINTHROP: But to begin what?

ELIDA: The drama.

WINTHROP: Drama? What sort of a drama?

ELIDA: Well, I guess you'd call it a romantic drama.

WINTHROP (*After a pause, frowning*): I trust there hasn't been any trouble with Alexander.

ELIDA (*With a short laugh*): Trouble!

WINTHROP (*Sternly*): Has he been bothering you, Elida?

ELIDA: He thinks I want to have an affair with him. (*Turning back around, coming out with it all now*) And Aunt Nellie's convinced that we *are*. Not only convinced, but revels in it. And Caroline's wild with suspicion, although not of me yet. Isn't it fantastic? And all over *nothing*, Winthrop!

WINTHROP (*Shaking his head*): Fantastic.

ELIDA: Wouldn't you think they had enough out of life without wanting me, too. It's indecent.

WINTHROP (*Nodding*): I suppose there's always something indecent about starvation. You see, they're starved, Elida. Starved for one little slice of genuine emotion. Oh, they've been snapping at each other for years, I know that, but they have no real appetite for themselves. They're too much alike. They want to sink their teeth into a *real* person.

ELIDA (*Surprised*): *Me?*

WINTHROP: Oh, you're tremendously real, my dear. Don't you know that? There's all sorts of emotion in you simmering below the surface. They can smell it. Like blood.

ELIDA (*After a pause*): I'd like to think that's a compliment.

WINTHROP: Of course it is. The greatest they could give you.

ELIDA (*Getting up*): Oh. I meant a compliment from you.

WINTHROP: From me? But you know *my* good opinion of you.

ELIDA: Do I? (*Walks about for a moment*) Well, the point is, what do I do about them. Now?

WINTHROP: I know what I'd do.

ELIDA: What?

WINTHROP (*Rather grimly*): They want a drama. I'd give them a drama. I'd give it to them until they begged me to stop. Until they went right down on their knees and begged me.

ELIDA: But how?

WINTHROP: Can you act?

ELIDA: Good heavens, no. (*Reflecting*) At least I've never tried.

WINTHROP: I bet you can. With all you have inside.

ELIDA: What would you have me act?

WINTHROP (*Serious*): The lover. The tremendous lover. You and Alexander are Anthony and Cleopatra! The world's your stage. You must tell your aunt. You must tell Caroline. You must lead him to them and blurt out your news.

This thing is too big to be secret! This thing is for everyone!

ELIDA: Winthrop! You're making fun of me!

WINTHROP (*Shaking his head*): I've never been more serious.
You could do it. I know you could. And can't you *see* what
it would do for them? Caroline with her peeking jealousy, and Aunt Nellie with her scatological assumptions,
and Alexander with his furtive pinching. Why it would
cleanse them! It would dignify them!

ELIDA (*Spellbound*): And then what would happen?

WINTHROP: Oh, nothing would happen. That's the point.
They'd simply be scared to death.

ELIDA: By me?

WINTHROP: Who else? They'd run like mice.

ELIDA: All of them? Even Alexander? After what I've
just told you? You're not very complimentary to my
charms.

WINTHROP: Oh, he's hot enough for a backstairs affair, sure.
But the prospect of an open break with the wife who sup-
ports him would send him scampering off as fast as his
little feet could carry him. Back to *both* his mothers.

ELIDA (*Pensive*): I see. It's really a perfect plan, isn't it? Except where does it leave the poor country cousin who's
just declared her great passion? I get packed off to Maine,
I guess. I'd be the cause of too much embarrassment,
wouldn't I? My little act might have given me ideas above
my station.

WINTHROP (*Shocked*): Oh, Elida, come now. I never meant
anything like that.

ELIDA: But you're so detached, Winthrop. You sit in your
arena box like a Roman senator and watch us poor gladi-

ators fighting below. Every now and then you may devise a new form of combat for us to engage in.

WINTHROP (*Really upset now*): Elida, I've hurt your feelings, and I'm very sorry. Please forget my whole silly idea. It was just a joke anyway. A bad one.

ELIDA (*Relenting*): Oh, it's not your fault. How could you know I was so steeped in . . . what's it called? The inertly sentimental condition? Who knows what I expected? Maybe I even dreamed you would sweep down on a great black charger and rescue me from Alexander.

(*Noise in the hall. Enter CAROLINE followed by a meeker ALEXANDER door C.*)

CAROLINE (*Casually*): Hi, Elida. Good evening, Winthrop. You're dining here? What a glutton you are for punishment.

WINTHROP (*Mildly reproving*): But I enjoy dining here, Caroline.

CAROLINE (*Sitting*): You do? Well, *chacun à son goût*, as I always say. It's perfectly extraordinary how many bachelors one sees in the houses of mothers-in-law. It must be a kind of penance they pay for their freedom.

ELIDA (*Nervous*): Would you like a cocktail, Caroline?

CAROLINE: No, dear, don't bother. I had one before I left.

ELIDA: It's no bother.

CAROLINE: You think *I* don't know? Fume and fuss, fume and fuss, and finally that ancient Alice emerges with one rather vermouthy martini on a silver tray. With a cherry in it.

ALEXANDER: Darling, that's not quite fair.

CAROLINE: Well, who wants to be fair? Tell me what we're in for, Elida. Who else is coming?

ELIDA: The Misses Harcrosse.

CAROLINE: I could have guessed that. Anyone else?

ELIDA: That's all.

CAROLINE (*Brightly*): Good. We shall be five women to two men. What Mrs. Hone would call a balanced party.

ELIDA: Well, Aunt Nellie did try to get Colonel Sturtevant, but he said he was too deaf for the opera now.

CAROLINE (*Sniffing*): As if that were an excuse. He could have had my place. But it makes no matter. After all, Miss Harriet Harcrosse can pass for a man. Did you tell her black tie?

ALEXANDER: Really, darling. Your tongue is very sharp tonight.

CAROLINE: But you know it's perfectly true, isn't it, Winthrop? The Harcrosses are like a married couple. Everyone knows that.

WINTHROP (*Ironically polite*): Do they indeed? Miss Emily, I take it, is the wife?

CAROLINE: Of course, you know (*she mimics her subject with gestures*), charming, irresponsible, ethereal, the *mad* soul. While Miss Harriet plays the gruff husband, the faithful watchdog, lovingly critical. Oh, keep your eye on them, Winthrop.

ELIDA (*Warningly*): Caroline, I heard the front door.

CAROLINE (*Her hand to her mouth*): Oops.

(*MISS EMILY and MISS HARRIET HARCROSSE appear at door C. in red and black velvet, respectively, their feet in pumps. Stout and elderly, they resemble each other in squareness of feature and grayness of hair, yet MISS EMILY, the effusive one, is characterized by her sweeping gestures, her habit of playing with her necklace of large pearls, while MISS HARRIET peers*)

at the room through the severe detachment of her sole adorn-
ment, a pince-nez. As they come in, the others rise. MRS. HONE
makes her belated appearance at door L. and approaches to meet
them.)

MRS. HONE: I'm sorry, all. I'm late. Emily, how are you?
Harriet? Good evening, Winthrop. Caroline. And my
own boy, my good one. (*She kisses ALEXANDER. There is*
a general shaking of hands before all sit.)

MISS EMILY: And dear Caroline, what *luck* to catch you and
Alexander free for a family evening. We hear from our
nieces how sought after the Alexander Hones are. (*She*
raises her hands.) Quite the popular couple, they say.

CAROLINE (*Glancing at her husband*): Yes, I've an idea Alexander *has* been rather sought after recently.

MRS. HONE (*Defensively, to Caroline*): I don't see how anyone
could be very sought after working as hard as he has to
work for your father, Caroline.

MISS EMILY (*Nervous, covering up the pause that ensues*): Oh,
the way the young people have to *work* these days! I don't
see how they stand it. Why, when Papa was in the railway
he used to come home for lunch every day. And drink
Madeira. It was a more civilized, a more gracious New
York.

MISS HARRIET: That was Grandpapa, Emily, and well before we were born. Papa always lunched at the Downtown.

MISS EMILY: Did he? Did he really? Dear me. (*Looking*
around the room for another subject) Well, goodness me,
does poor Winthrop have to escort *four* ladies tonight?
I'll bet he's dying, right now.

WINTHROP: I'm bearing up, Miss Emily.

MISS EMILY (*With a little scream*): Bearing up? Is *that* modern-day gallantry? It wasn't that way when we were girls, was it, Harriet?

MISS HARRIET: Personally, I've always found the gallantry of the so-called stronger sex a much overrated thing.

MISS EMILY: Oh, Harriet. You *devil*. (*Turning to MRS. HONE*) You know what she was telling me tonight, Nellie? She keeps records of everything. This will be our fortieth *Tristan*.

MISS HARRIET: *My* fortieth, Emily. Your thirty-ninth. You remember, you missed one that winter you had the milk leg.

MISS EMILY (*Shocked*): Harriet, *please*. (*To MRS. HONE*) Who's singing tonight, Nellie?

MRS. HONE: Gluckin.

MISS EMILY (*With a shrug*): Oh, Gluckin. All very well, I suppose, but hardly Flagstad.

MRS. HONE (*Firmly, reverently*): But there's never been anyone to touch Flagstad.

MISS EMILY: Why, Nellie, have you forgotten Ternina? Ternina who was pure *magic!*

MISS HARRIET: Fremstad was your favorite, Emily. I remember distinctly.

MISS EMILY (*With authority, as if to close the subject*): Of course, *Papa* used to say that if you hadn't heard Lily Lehmann, you hadn't heard Isolde.

CAROLINE (*Bored*): I wonder what *his* papa used to say. Jenny Lind?

(*MISS HARRIET and MRS. HONE glare at CAROLINE, and MISS EMILY, still the peacemaker, again tries to fill the gap.*)

MISS EMILY (*With a coy glance at ELIDA*): Did you know, Nellie, that Elida and I share a taste for a different kind of music?

MRS. HONE (*Gruffly*): What kind?

MISS EMILY: A lighter kind. Oh, it's not that we aren't loyal Wagnerians, Nellie. You don't have to look at me that way. We're tried and true. But we still have a sneaking nostalgia for the music hall. Don't we, Elida?

ELIDA (*Confused*): The music hall?

MISS EMILY: I was referring to my glimpse of you last summer at what I believe is called a "folly."

(*ELIDA gives a little gasp, and CAROLINE looks up.*)

MRS. HONE: Do you go to the follies, Emily? Harriet, I'm surprised you let her.

MISS EMILY (*Delighted to be considered daring*): Oh, Harriet went, too. We'd come into town for poor Daisy Livermore's funeral, and it was a scorching night. They told us at the Colony Club that the theater was aircooled, so I gave Harriet a look and said (*Coyly*), "Why not?"

MRS. HONE: And what was it called, this folly?

MISS EMILY (*Turning to her sister*): What *was* it called, Harriet?

MISS HARRIET: *The Ballad Girl.*

(*ELIDA looks down quickly, and CAROLINE and MRS. HONE stare at each other.*)

CAROLINE (*In a dry, sarcastic tone, to MISS EMILY*): You've told us who lured Miss Harriet on this radical evening. Could you by any chance tell us who lured your fellow Wagnerian, Elida?

MISS EMILY (*Surprised at her tone*): No, I didn't see who she was with. It was just a glimpse through the crowd. Was it you, Caroline?

CAROLINE: No. It was not I. (*To ELIDA*) Was it by any chance that fellow Wagnerian, my husband?

ALEXANDER: Now wait a second, Caroline, I can explain all that.

CAROLINE (*Sharp*): I'm asking Elida!

ELIDA (*Nervous*): Why, yes. I don't know who else would have taken me.

MRS. HONE (*Coming heavily to the rescue*): And why not, Caroline? Wasn't it a good cousinly act on my boy's part?

CAROLINE (*Ominously bright*): Certainly. It's just that I'm envious, that's all. *The Ballad Girl* happens to be something that I particularly wanted to see myself. As I believe I told you both this afternoon. In my naiveté.

ALEXANDER (*Anxious*): But you were away, Caroline. Anyway, I'd love to go again. It's well worth seeing twice.

CAROLINE (*Coldly*): Perhaps. Except, of course, I wouldn't dream of asking you to take me *now*.

MRS. HONE (*Angrily*): You go to everything in the season, Caroline. Poor Elida has no fun at all, cooped up with an old woman like myself. Must you begrudge her one musical?

CAROLINE (*Rising*): It doesn't sound to me, Mrs. Hone, as though Elida is so terribly cooped up. And when she is, I'm sure she likes it. With my husband coming in every day on the excuse of seeing you! Good god, it's too degrading to contemplate!

ELIDA: Caroline, what are you *saying?*

ALEXANDER: You can't speak that way to Mother!

(*MRS. HONE suddenly leans forward, clutching her chest.*)

MRS. HONE: My heart! It's my heart again!

(*General consternation*)

WINTHROP (*Hurrying to MRS. HONE's side*): Cousin Nellie, can I help you? (*To ELIDA*) Will you call the doctor?

ELIDA (*Pulling herself together, taking charge*): Wait. It's only one of her spells. I know what to do. (*Going over to MRS. HONE, she takes a pill quickly from the silver box at the table by her side and gives it to her. To the others*) Please, she'll be all right. Go into the dining room and start dinner, will you all? Winthrop, please take them in.

ALEXANDER: Are you sure she's all right?

ELIDA: Quite sure. Please go in now. She likes to be alone when this happens.

(*The others move slowly out door R., glancing nervously at MRS. HONE as they do so.*)

ELIDA (*Alone with MRS. HONE, feels her pulse*): Aunt Nellie, are you feeling better? How is it now?

MRS. HONE (*Lifting her head slowly and looking at ELIDA hard for a moment*): Go with him. Go off with him.

ELIDA (*Shocked*): With Alexander?

MRS. HONE: You see how she treats us. You see what she thinks of us. She hates us. Free him, Elida! Take him away! Don't let her *win*.

ELIDA: You seem to forget that he's not mine to go off with. He has two children. He has responsibilities.

MRS. HONE (*Grunting*): Love. It wasn't that way when I was a girl. My aunt Augusta gave up everything for Prince Mantowski. It was the world well lost. Or can't you young people understand that? (*Sneering*) And you pretend to understand *Tristan*.

ELIDA (*Trying to make light of it*): But I haven't had a love potion. I believe Isolde behaved quite respectably before she had hers.

MRS. HONE (*Snorting*): Respectably. That's all any of you care about. Can you *eat* respectability?

ELIDA: Don't you think you'd better go to bed now? I can bring you something on a tray.

MRS. HONE: A tray? And have Caroline sit at the head of my table? Not likely. I'm going in.

ELIDA: Oh, Aunt Nellie. Please! I can't bear it.

MRS. HONE: If I can bear it, you can. What are you young for, anyway?

(*She gets up very slowly, and ELIDA helps her toward door R. Just as they reach it, it opens and CAROLINE appears.*)

CAROLINE (*Surprised*): Oh. Are you feeling better?

MRS. HONE (*Snorting*): I'll live. Small thanks to your manners tonight, Caroline.

CAROLINE: I came out to speak to Elida.

MRS. HONE (*Crossly*): We're all going to dine now. It can wait.

CAROLINE: I'm sorry, Mrs. Hone. It can't wait. I'll keep her only a few minutes.

MRS. HONE (*To ELIDA*): Shall I leave you with her, child?

ELIDA: If she wants. Are you all right?

MRS. HONE (*Shrugging*): Oh, I'm indestructible. It'll take more than Caroline to do me in.

(*Exit MRS. HONE door R. CAROLINE closes the door after her.*)

CAROLINE (*After a pause*): I suppose we may as well sit down.

ELIDA: Yes.

(*They sit. CAROLINE lights a cigarette and puffs at it. ELIDA, absolutely still, looks at the floor.*)

CAROLINE: I don't so much mind your borrowing my husband, Elida Rodman. As long as it's quite understood between us that I shall be wanting him back.

(*Pause as ELIDA, now looking down at her hands, says nothing.*)

There are a lot of things I could say that I won't. I think it might be sufficient if I pointed out that you were hired to be his mother's companion. (*With a wry smile*) Not his.

(*ELIDA still says nothing.*)

Do you hear me? (*Sharply*) I'm speaking to you, Elida!

ELIDA (*Looking up*): Do you really deduce all this, Caroline, from the fact that Alexander was once kind enough to take me to the theater?

CAROLINE (*Sniffing*): You may have heard of archaeologists who are able to reconstruct the skeleton of a dinosaur from a single bone of its toe. There you are. Except my discovery turns out not to be a dinosaur at all. It's only a rather small mouse.

(*ELIDA looks away. She appears to be concentrating on something else.*)

A mouse, I said. (*Angrily*) Don't keep pretending you haven't heard me, Elida!

ELIDA (*Turning back to her, with the calm of one who has just made a final decision*): All right, Caroline. I *have* heard you. I was only wondering if you were capable of discussing such a delicate matter as a civilized and sophisticated woman should.

CAROLINE (*Her eyes widen at this impudence.*): Oh? And have you decided?

ELIDA: Yes. (*Nodding*) I think, on the whole, you are.

CAROLINE: Thank you!

ELIDA (*In a new tone, tense, but with increased assurance as she goes ahead*): What has happened to Alexander and me is not, I suppose, unusual. But to the individuals involved it must always seem like a minor miracle.

CAROLINE (*Staring*): What do you mean?

ELIDA: Simply that we're in love, Caroline. Sublimely, even ridiculously in love.

CAROLINE (*Sitting up*): Are you *mad*?

ELIDA (*Shaking her head, as if in half-regretful assent*): Oh, yes. Quite mad, I'm afraid. We both are.

CAROLINE: No, no, you don't see what I mean. I mean *you* may have some feeling, yes, I suppose that would be only natural, but Alexander, well, after all . . . (*She trails off with an elaborate shrug.*)

ELIDA (*Clearly*): After all *what*, Caroline?

CAROLINE (*Now condescending*): Well, after all, my poor Elida, I don't deny he may have paid you some little attention—I know how *he* is—but to construct a *grande passion* out of a few winks and passes, well, really, my dear, you don't want to make an utter fool of yourself, do you?

ELIDA (*Noble, dignified*): There were no winks or passes, Caroline. Alexander and I understood each other from the first. It was love, just like that. Very pure and very simple.

CAROLINE (*Snorting*): That's what you say.

ELIDA (*Unyielding*): That's what he says.

CAROLINE (*Startled*): Alexander? He said *that*?

ELIDA: Of course he said it, Caroline. Do you think I'm making this up? He's said it dozens of times, he to me and I to him, whispered it, shouted it—

CAROLINE: Shouted it!

ELIDA (*Nodding*): Even shouted it.

CAROLINE (*Scared now, shifting her method of attack*): Look, my dear, let's be practical. Just for a moment. Assuming that you and Alexander have had . . . well, some sort of a thing about each other, even assuming you've been lovers—I don't know, the Hones are queer people—what sort of future do you think there could possibly be in it?

ELIDA: I suppose that must depend very largely on the attitude you take.

CAROLINE: *I* take!

ELIDA: That's what Alexander says. I myself can hardly believe that you will wish to hold a man who has so clearly demonstrated—if you will forgive the expression—his preference.

CAROLINE (*Outraged*): His preference! Of all the impudence! You can't seriously believe that a man in Alexander's position will want to go on with this? Now?

ELIDA: Why not?

CAROLINE: When his wife knows?

ELIDA (*Coolly*): But of course it was inevitable that you should know. From the very beginning. I always told him that.

CAROLINE (*Her eyes bulging*): You can't really think . . . oh, no, that would be impossible.

ELIDA (*Calmly*): Can't think what, Caroline?

CAROLINE: You can't *really* think that Alexander would leave his wife and children for you? (*Letting herself go*) A country cousin from Maine?

ELIDA (*Quietly*): It won't do you any good to call me names, Caroline. Surely you owe it to yourself to be rational.

CAROLINE (*Almost in a scream*): Rational! You have the nerve to sit there and say I should be rational! (*She pauses to swal-*

low and has time to reflect on the vulnerability of her own position.) We'll see who's the more rational. Let us suppose for a moment that Alexander were free to marry you. How would you live? You're probably too much in the clouds to face these small realities. You see how Alexander and I live now, and you've probably assumed, as people like you always assume, that he's the breadwinner. Well, he's not. The money's mine, Miss Rodman. All mine. Alexander has nothing but his salary at my father's bank and a small trust fund. I doubt if the salary would survive the divorce, and you couldn't live on the trust. And I wouldn't count on his mother, either. She's been eating into her capital for years. It must be largely gone by now.

ELIDA (*Smiling imperturbably*): That kind of thing, Caroline, means less than nothing to Alexander and me.

CAROLINE: To you, possibly. You've always been a pauper. But Alexander, I think you'll find, is a horse of a different color.

ELIDA (*Defiant*): Ask him! You'll see.

(*CAROLINE's eyes follow ELIDA's nervously to door R.*)

Ask him!

(*CAROLINE gets up and goes suddenly to door R., which she opens.*)

CAROLINE (*Hoarsely*): Alexander! Alexander, come in here, will you?

ALEXANDER (*Appearing in door R.*): Caroline, is there something wrong? Why do you look at me like that? (*He enters and closes the door hastily behind him.*)

CAROLINE (*In a rasping tone*): Elida says you're in love with her. She says you want to leave me and go off with her. Is it true?

ALEXANDER (*Horror-struck, turning to ELIDA*): *Elida!* What have you been *saying?* Have you taken leave of your senses?

ELIDA (*Reaching out her arms to him*): Alexander, darling, you don't have to conceal it anymore. We're free now. *Free!*

ALEXANDER (*His eyes bulging*): You'll have to excuse her, Caroline. She must be sick.

ELIDA (*Rising to heights*): But, dearest, we're beyond all that! Way beyond! Don't you *see?* It isn't a thing anymore of holding hands on the sly or lingering in doorways. It's broken its fetters, it's smashed through everything, it's *out!* And *I'm* not ashamed. I'm proud of it. Proud of loving and being loved by you!

ALEXANDER: Caroline, the girl's out of her mind! She's been working too hard. She's misconstrued the cousinly interest I've always felt it my duty to take in her into something quite different.

CAROLINE: *Quite* different, I agree. (*Calmer now, she looks slowly from him to ELIDA.*) Have you really inspired such a love, Alexander? And without even meaning to? (*Shaking her head*) If that is so, you must have something in you that I have evidently failed to appreciate. Has this poor girl really come to believe that you'd walk out on me and the children and your job for her?

ALEXANDER: Caroline, I never told her any such thing! I swear it!

CAROLINE: I do believe that you never said it. (*A pause*) And I do believe that you never meant to. (*Changing her tone*) Well, shall we leave it at that? And join the Misses Harcrosse for their rudely interrupted meal? What *must* they be thinking?

ALEXANDER: Caroline, after this grueling scene can't we go quietly home? I can't face the prospect of *Tristan*.

CAROLINE (*Coolly*): But I can. I feel like King Mark. Except maybe nothing has happened. His long solo at the end of the second act will give me a chance to think over how you and I might come to a better understanding of each other. We seem to need it.

(*CAROLINE returns to the dining room followed by ALEXANDER and, after a moment's delay, ELIDA.*)

Scene 3

SCENE: *Same, five hours later*
(*Enter MRS. HONE, followed by ELIDA and WINTHROP.*)

MRS. HONE: It was good of you to see us home, Winthrop. But you didn't have to come upstairs.

WINTHROP: Elida offered me a nightcap, Cousin Nellie.

MRS. HONE (*Faintly surprised*): Did she? Very well then. I'll take myself to bed. You young things can stay up all night if you choose. It wasn't a bad evening, after all, though it started so badly with Caroline acting up about that musical comedy. I thought we might be in for a real scandal. But then it seemed to simmer down. And during the Lieberstod, which was wonderfully sung tonight, I wondered if it wasn't better, after all, to leave these domestic dramas on the stage where they belong.

ELIDA: Much better, Aunt Nellie. At home we need peace.

MRS. HONE: And an old busybody like myself had better find it in her bed, is that what you mean, my dear? Well, good night. (*Exit MRS. HONE door L. ELIDA and WINTHROP look at each other for a minute.*)

ELIDA: I suppose congratulations are in order.

WINTHROP: For what?

ELIDA: For what I told you in the entr'acte, of course. I played your little scene, and it worked out just as you predicted.

WINTHROP: With such an actress in the leading role, how could it fail? I only wish I had been there to watch it.

ELIDA: What makes you so sure I was acting?

WINTHROP: How do you mean?

ELIDA: Do you completely assume that I could never have been attracted to Alexander myself?

WINTHROP: Completely.

ELIDA: What makes you so sure?

WINTHROP: In the first place, because he's such an ass. And in the second because I suspect you might be just a bit in love with *me*.

ELIDA (*After a pause*): Do you think arrogance is always appealing?

WINTHROP (*Surprised*): Arrogance? Why is that arrogance? Ah, yes, of course. You call it that because I haven't told you the rest of the story.

ELIDA (*Sarcastic*): It couldn't be, could it, that you're in love with *me*? (*He bows.*) Oh, Winthrop, can't you ever be serious? Ever?

WINTHROP: I'm quite serious.

ELIDA: I wonder if you even know what the word means. If that sober demeanor doesn't hide the greatest cynic in New York.

WINTHROP: You flatter me. But even a cynic, provided I were that, can be in love, can't he? (*A pause*) It all happened quite suddenly after another evening in your aunt's opera box. It was *Tosca*. I was sitting behind you and found myself comparing the romantic life of the heroine with your dry imprisonment in Cousin Nellie's art-stuffed existence. I became upset. When I got home I sat in my living room to look at my porcelains and relax my nerves. But calm eluded me. My pulses throbbed. And then, quite suddenly—bang!—I saw that the whole thing that was wrong with me, or should I say right with me, was you. I slapped the table before me very hard, involuntarily, and broke my small robin's egg Ming vase in pieces.

ELIDA (*Awed*): Oh!

WINTHROP: And do you know something? I didn't care at all. I loved you, Elida. I love you now. Don't you think you ought to marry me after smashing my Ming?

ELIDA: It's that bad?

WINTHROP: That bad.

ELIDA: I'll have to think about it then. But it's really almost too neat, isn't it? Your little scheme so beautifully worked out. Alexander and Caroline will settle down to a more realistic marriage, he cured, at least for a time, from his wandering eye, and she, relieved not to have lost him and resolved, we hope, to be less nasty in the future. And Aunt Nellie reconciled to their reunion and comforted to have a scandal averted which she had wanted only in fantasy. And finally the poor country cousin awarded the hand of the wealthy hero.

WINTHROP (*Laughing*): It's always been said in social circles that I was the type to marry someone for her money. Now look what's happening. Someone's going to marry me for mine!

ELIDA: People who play with other people's lives are lucky if they get married at all. Go home now, Winthrop, but call me before you go to sleep. I may have something to tell you.

(WINTHROP takes his immediate departure, blowing her a kiss, and MRS. HONE looms in the door L.)

MRS. HONE *(Suspicious)*: Has he gone already? What have you two been hatching?

ELIDA: We've been planning the future, Aunt Nellie.

MRS. HONE: What future? Won't we all go on just the same? In our own dreary way?

ELIDA: Not quite in the same dreary way. At least I hope not. Certainly I hope not for myself.

MRS. HONE: You? What do you think you're going to do?

ELIDA: I'm going to marry Winthrop DeLancey.

MRS. HONE *(Aghast)*: Winthrop! You? You've taken leave of your senses, girl.

ELIDA: I hope not, Aunt Nellie.

MRS. HONE *(Collapsing)*: Elida, tell your old aunt you're only fooling!

ELIDA: No, Aunt Nellie. I've been fooling all day. Now I've stopped.

MRS. HONE: And what's to become of me, I'd like to know? Who's to look after me?

ELIDA: Caroline.

MRS. HONE *(Wailing)*: Caroline! You leave me to Caroline? Lay out my old bones for the hyena? Is this your gratitude, Elida Rodman?

ELIDA: Among Paleolithics, Aunt Nellie, is there such a thing as gratitude?

End

FICTION   Auchincloss, Louis.
Auchincl
           The friend of women
           and other stories.

                              685797
$24.00   02/27/2007

DATE